CRONE

By Azalee Wolfe

MAGPIE HOUSE

CRONE

Copyright © 2017 Azalee Wolfe

Cover art by Chasing Color Studios

First Edition published by Magpie House April 2017

USA

ISBN-13: 978-0-9986925-0-0

Dedicated to all those who help me obsess over each and every thing I run across as I explore a book in progress.

Thank you to my husband, who watches the everyday world fall apart around me while I get lost in the words and helps me find my way back again.

CHAPTER ONE

The sign said the name of the shop was The Rookery. A painted raven, head slightly cocked to the side, weighed each visitor before allowing them entrance. Every antique buyer dreams of finding a hole-in-the-wall place like the Rookery. The problem wasn't so much that it was hard to find; the problem was finding it twice. It was easy to look past. The windows were filmed over like sightless eyes, soiled with nostalgia and layers of dust and nicotine. Once inside, it looked like any other antique store. Jumbles of strangers' memories, with no real sense of time as each decade's refuse patiently gained enough age to become precious again. Each item belonged to the time that created it, like a child to a parent, but here everything tumbled together until the years stopped making any sense. A toy from the fifties rested right beside a set of books from the eighties and an old cracked Edwardian era dish that had been mislabeled. Trays of jewelry lay on the top of available surfaces, with nothing to help distinguish which pieces were worth looking at.

The Rookery was laid out like a house, though it seemed unlikely anyone had ever lived in it. The rooms were too tiny to have served as decent bedrooms, but a perfect size to display treasures. Kass had updated the layout, and each room had a theme. It was far better, Jezi had to admit, than it had been in the dusty days when she had mainly stored things in random piles. She had owned and lived in the shop for decades. Now, the Rookery had the stamp of Kass's charm. The kitchen, with no running water of course, looked functional with antique appliances intact. More than one person had tried to buy them from her through the years. He had removed the cabinet doors to display everything inside, mismatched dishes stacked in various states of chipped and crazed and cracked. Wooden counters gleamed; many a year had passed since anything had been prepared on them, but Kass kept them in beautiful condition, sanding and oiling them to perfection. Decorative plates hung on racks along the walls, handwritten price stickers in the corners. Bright sunshine and jumbled memories filled the room.

In the next room over, a tiny bed sat in the farthest corner, complete with miniature bedset of dust ruffles, pillow shams, and a tiny down comforter folded at the foot. Beside the bed sat a doll version, complete to every detail. The set wasn't for sale; though again, many people had tried. Toys covered every available surface of the room, on shelves and inside boxes. The toys came from every era, but looked so natural together that most overlooked what might otherwise stand out.

Kass had designed rooms devoted to trains, rooms for lace, rooms for jewelry and dress clothing, and rooms for rugs. There were so many rooms that one had to wonder how this building was so much bigger inside than it appeared. Yaga had always assured curious customers it was just an illusion. The size of the rooms, she would explain. They would nod, appeased for the moment, but leave confused. Jezi would chuckle, because she knew they had only seen the front half of the building.

If someone looked hard enough they might find treasures far eclipsing the garage sale trash offered by many so-called antique stores. Each row contained secrets to divulge to those who could see the truth hidden under layers of time and grime. The shop rarely saw any customers; those who did come didn't stay long, and those who purchased never found their way back. Jezi walked among the trash and treasures equally: each loved, all intimately known. As she passed, she held her hand over the items, dipping lower and angling higher to keep her hand level, mumbling to herself. The process resembled a benediction. She went by Jezi, a shorter version of one of her names. She didn't use her full name anymore, never had liked it. Jezi was a tiny, older woman, her age impossible to pin down. She looked brittle with old age, but she stood straight and gave the impression somehow that she was indestructible. She was a foul-mouthed firecracker with a nasty sarcastic bite: short-tempered, intelligent, and witty.

"Jezi." She ignored him. "Jez." She had no intention of interrupting her work to address whatever problem he had concocted. "Bab—" She interrupted him quickly, before he had a chance to get the whole name out.

"What?" She snapped at him from below. Kass was ridiculously tall. He wasn't only tall, he was gaunt. Hollow, shadowed cheekbones and sunken eyes betrayed his age, almost as old as herself. He wore a black button down and sharply creased pants. Polished shoes winked at her flirtatiously through a mist of freshly applied aftershave. Jezi rolled her eyes. They made an oddly mismatched couple, though it had never been like that between them. They were closer to brother and sister if they were anything at all.

"I'll wager you're here to ask for time off. You can't work the shop because you have plans." Every sign indicated that he had plans for tonight, plans that included female company. The amount of female attention he could scrounge up mystified her. He was not handsome, far from it, but he did have an indefinable charisma. Whatever it was, his spell didn't work on Jezi. They had known each other too long, too much history between them. Neither remembered how they met.

He didn't even have the decency to pretend embarrassment. "Jez," he wheedled, "you know you don't actually need me to work." He waved his hand dismissively in the direction of the well-stocked antiquities. Every time someone showed up to the Rookery, Jezi had to face the possibility that a potential customer would choose one of her treasures to take home. She wasn't in the business to make money or to unload the inventory in her shop. She wasn't particularly motivated to sell any of her items; rather, she would have been physically pained to lose even one of them.

Each item housed in the Rookery represented a memory, more than a lifetime's worth. Once upon a time, what felt like a hundred years ago, people had called her Grandmother, though she had never been the milk-and-cookies type. Thin and wiry, Jezi was as strong as she had ever been, as though age honed her like a weapon. She didn't eat like an old woman either; she had a ferocious appetite, preferring steak, roast chicken, pork chops, cutlets, anything over the pastries and salads that she saw other old women eating.

Jezi's shop was remarkably hard to find, a fact that she was proud of. She took care of it, in her own way. This way did not include keeping it orderly or clean, but it did involve keeping a schedule. She and Kass were the only ones who worked; Jezi didn't keep anyone else in her employ – mostly because she didn't have to pay Kass. It was about the only thing working in his favor these days. More evenings than not, he ducked out on feigned business, or he was a little too eager to run long-winded errands for her.

All of Kass's nonsense aside, tomorrow Jezi had plans to take the day off to have lunch with two of her friends. Kass would have to mind the shop in her absence, and she would enjoy some long-windedness of her own. Jezi put on her sweetest smile and turned back to Kass.

"Kass, you go right ahead. You go make that little sweetheart's night. Bring her something shiny, or something with petals. Those young ones like that." Kass narrowed his eyes slightly at her, trying to untangle her tone from her meaning. He didn't trust her when she went all syrupy like this. "Go ahead, pick one of the newer antique rings. Find a color she likes. Tell her some story about how it came from a wealthy estate." She motioned toward the ring trays, swishing her hands and walking towards him, effectively herding him.

He snagged a likely candidate, sure that Jezi had already thought of a way to make him pay. She raised an eyebrow at his first choice, so he hovered over a few other choices before choosing a little pearl number. His date was less likely to love this little gem, but he would do better to enjoy Jezi's offer than to turn down her unusual show of generosity – no matter the motivation. He slipped the bauble into a pocket and made his way out the door. Jezi watched him leave; the sky was already turning cloudy and grey, the wind picking up. It would be an unseasonably cold night.

She was honestly looking forward to lunch with her friends the next day, mostly because of Morgana. By herself, Keris could be too stuffy, too grandmotherly, for Jezi's taste. Morgana and Jezi had been friends for more years than she could count. They hadn't always been friendly, but it seemed that was often the way of it between women. They had become a tight set, the three of them, closer to sisters than friends. Right now, Keris and she were not exactly friendly, but with Morgana there it would be pleasant enough.

With Kass gone, the wind howling outside, and an empty shop to tend, Jezi settled her shelves, patting things back into place after all the pacing of the day. She did some dusting, stirring up tiny clouds of ancient accumulation to drift around the room before settling back in for the night. It was more of a chance for everything to breathe than a cleaning. She moved up and down rows and in and out of tiny purposeless rooms, creaking over the worn floors. Jezi turned off the lights, casting a last look across the shop; it seemed that she gazed over a thousand children, tucked in and sleeping for another night.

Jezi's house connected to the shop by a door and a daunting passageway. Should a customer end up lost or looking for a restroom, which Jezi didn't offer anyway, the hall was long enough and dark enough to spook them back out into the store. She did get customers after all, but did her best to make sure that they didn't return for future visits. Not offering a bathroom was apparently a great step in that direction. She liked the long hallway; it helped break the connection between work life and home life.

The house itself looked older than the front. The walls were white, but constructed of wood and painted. The floors were the same wood as the shop out front, though considerably more worn. Jezi preferred natural light to electric, leaving candles around for emergencies, the rooms lit by oil lamps and fireplaces. The city seemed cold so frequently, which she chalked up to the age of her bones in these times.

For many years, Jezi had lived far from the cities, out among the trees and the sky and the wildness. She missed it sometimes. Those days had been before Kass had come to live with her, though they had known each other in the old country. They had moved over together, becoming much closer in their shared separation. Jezi spent most of her time alone in those days. That part, she did not miss. She hadn't been young even then and wasn't sure that she remembered a time when she had been. Youth seemed more like a foreign country than a time in her own past.

Everything Jezi had ever owned still lived in the Rookery somewhere, and it had been a long interesting life. She had decided, a while back, to make her life less interesting. She wandered, restless tonight, much the same as she had wandered through the shop. Sleep felt far away, so she parked herself in front of the fireplace with a book. The cat sauntered in, but he wasn't the type of cat to curl up in a lap. Jezi eyed him warily. They had entered a certain level of truce, but she still didn't quite trust Bayun's claws, especially these days. The cat was older now as well, and his claws didn't retract anymore. It meant that sometimes he needed help, though he wasn't happy about it, to untangle himself from chairs and carpets. Bayun settled across the room, winking at her one eye at a time.

Jezi woke up the next morning still sitting in her chair. The fire had burned out sometime in the night, which explained why she was so stiff. She shuffled around getting the fire started again and then moved to the stove to start it up too. She hated the cold, the way it settled in her joints, and slept in her bones. She had to get the blood moving in the morning before the stiffness and pain would recede, but the fire helped. She hovered between the fireplace and the antique stove, stretching out to let the warmth soak in. Bayun was nowhere to be seen, probably off to find someplace warmer while she slept. *Stupid cat, couldn't even be bothered to sleep on her lap and keep them both warm.* They had never liked each other, which made her wonder why she still had the damn thing.

Coffee percolating in the kitchen, fires blazing in the hearths, Jezi began her day. She was meeting the girls for tea, she remembered, or she would be as soon as Kass showed up for work. He was late, as usual. He sauntered in about an hour after the shop opened, winking at her conspiratorially from the doorway. She grimaced back at him, less of a smile and more a baring of teeth. He had the good sense to wince. Kass had obviously had a good night; he was always healthier the next morning, the damn vampire. Just looking at his geriatrically happy face was making her grumpier.

"I have a lunch today," she snapped. "I am going to be late if I do not leave in the next five minutes. Nice of you to show up." He settled into a corner to preen, obviously proud of himself. He nodded at her, grinning more now. "Could you manage to have some clothes on still when I get back?" His grin split open, revealing crooked teeth. Kass had a bad habit of losing clothes on a good day; the better mood he was in, the more likely he was going to be semi-naked when she got back. It was annoyingly, awkwardly true. He had some crazy idea that he was more powerful the less clothes he had on. She was convinced that he was at least part-time crazy. There were days that he seemed normal, and then there were days like today, when he came in with that look on his face. *It was a good thing they rarely saw customers,* she sighed to herself. She slammed the door on her way out, much to his amusement. His croaking laughter rang out in the room behind her.

Determined to shake off Kass's crazy, Jezi headed for her favorite part of any day. She had lived much of her life without a vehicle at all, walking anywhere she needed to go. She had ridden in, and sometimes even owned cars, but she had never loved them. Cars were too big, too closed in, not enough air to breathe. The only benefit of a car, to her mind, was that they came with the best heaters in the world. The scooter definitely didn't have a heater, but it made up for it by going ridiculously fast. She never felt more free, more wild, than she did on that scooter. She wrapped her grey hair up, tucking in the free strands so they didn't whip against her ears and forehead. She even had a heavy leather jacket so that she wouldn't freeze, drawing away from her enjoyment of the experience. She did so hate to be cold.

She climbed on the back of the scooter, which should have been too big for her to control, but Jezi was stronger than she seemed. She loved the looks she got as she raced through traffic, an old woman on the back of a bike, bundled up in leathers. She had gone to buy a moped that day, and fell in love with a Shadow. The salesman hadn't been all that supportive, but he didn't want to lose the sale either, so she left on the Shadow instead of the little moped. She had never regretted that choice. Riding her Shadow felt like flying, and she never had cared what other people thought.

She pulled up and parked the bike, walking into the restaurant where her friends were waiting. She soaked up the stares, drawing something close to power from the awe with which people watched her. She loved the stares almost as much as she loved riding the bike itself. Once inside, she scanned the tables looking for Morgana. Not seeing Morgana's black-haired head, Jezi kicked herself for not taking longer. She didn't want to sit at a table with Keris, waiting for Morgana to show up, making awkward conversation.

Keris was a Grandmother, in every sense of the word. She wore her white hair pinned up in old-fashioned styles, still soft and gently curled. Jezi's own iron-grey hair felt more like wires than hair. Keris had a musical voice and skin that looked lit from within; the woman practically glowed. The beauty wasn't what made Jezi's hackles stand up, that was just a part of who Keris was. It was the way that she acted tranquil when Jezi knew different.

Just as Jezi decided to duck into the ladies' room to wait it out, Keris spotted her and waved her over to the table. Jezi groaned inwardly and walked quickly towards Keris, who was practically singing her name.

"Jez! Jez! Over here, sweetie, I'm over here!"

"I see you, Keris," she hissed, sliding into a seat. At least it was a table instead of a booth. Keris preferred the coziness of booths, insisting that they were a tiny hiding place, a chance for friends to create their own little world again. It was exactly what Jezi did not like about booths. She didn't like to sit hip-to-hip with anyone, elbows bumping as neighbors struggled to eat without eating in unison. She hated when people lifted their glasses at exactly the same time, an unspoken table signal.

Keris never seemed to notice; her happiness didn't depend on anyone but herself. She liked to wear diamonds, ice as she laughingly called them. She wore pristine, blinding white, and her hair was white, never veering into the yellowed tone seen on so many old women. Her porcelain skin was so pale that blue veins traced visible patterns beneath. The other reason Jezi didn't like her, despite their sisterly connection, was her affinity for the cold. Keris didn't love the cold to spite Jezi, despite what the old woman thought; she thrived in it like a glittering polar bear. Morgana always teased that she was the Winter Queen; Keris loved that, so now she said it about herself. Where Jezi looked older with every passing day, Keris wore her age gracefully. It wasn't that she didn't look old—she did, but her age didn't affect her beauty or her happiness. Jezi hadn't quite figured out that secret yet. Keris glowed and laughed and glided through life, refusing to let anything dim her internal light. It made Jezi crazy; she couldn't put her finger on why.

It could be that old age was easier on Keris because she had money: furs, diamonds, greyhounds, a lakehouse. Keris and her husband had raised two children, a boy and a girl, who had long since moved out. Jezi had never had any family of her own. *Maybe it changed the way age seeped into every angle of your life*, she mused. Jezi had always had what she needed and never put any thought to it.

They small talked, and Jezi couldn't remember from one

sentence to the next what they talked about. Which was fine as Keris didn't need her to say much; she did enough talking for both of them. She had always been a strong willed woman, and she was capable of carrying on an intelligent conversation for at least three people at a time.

Morgana, on the other hand, was a contradictory force of nature. She was beautiful, but not elegant like Keris. The youngest of the trio, Morgana wore her hair black as a raven's wing, though her face betrayed her age. She had a violent temper, a wicked sense of humor, and Jezi loved her to distraction. Jezi loved Morgana's attitude towards her age, in that she had no attitude about it at all. She carried herself as though still thirty, or forty, or fifty; she was indefinable. Jezi knew what she liked about Morgana better than what she didn't like about Keris. Morgana was a rebel, a youthful spirit, independent, and she wasn't afraid to come face to face with the darker aspects of life.

Morgana blew in like a storm. The whole restaurant stopped to look at her; she was magnetic, one of those personalities who could play a flute and convince every person in her path to pied-piper right out the door with her. Conversations stopped, and Morgana moved through their wake, seemingly oblivious to the attention. She wandered through the tables, winding through worshipful eyes.

Morgana sat at the table, laughter in her eyes. "Afternoon sisters."

"You are impossible, Morgana," Jezi told her.

"I'm sure I don't have a clue what you mean."

"You do, and you know it!"

"But you love me. And you know it."

They didn't get together as often now as they used to. There was a time when nothing could come between the three of them—sisters in all but blood. There was an even older time, when they were too similar, more enemies than anything else. They all ordered food, not that any of them ate much anymore. It was nice actually, made paying for lunch easier. After food, all three women settled in to talk.

"You do it for the attention. You love the adoration. Speaking of —you're looking awfully *young* today, Morgana. I know you're almost as old as I am, so where is this coming from?" Jezi needled her friend.

"I like to change things up, that's all. Why show up the same way every day if you don't have to? I miss the old days, girls." This from Morgana, the self-assured, the ageless. Jezi was shocked.

"Why?"she asked bluntly. "The days when you were young, those were hard days. Now, though you greet the day with an older body, the world is so much improved." Surely Keris would understand Jezi's position on this. The old days, with everything they had had, were nothing compared to the way the world worked now.

"I wouldn't give up all of the new we have now, I just wish for more of what we had then. All of this is simply frosting, convenience. I miss the way things used to be. I want to try something, and I need both of you to help me. We won't be able to do this at any of our usual haunts, so I need you both to meet me tomorrow night at my home." The other two women at the table stared at Morgana: Keris with confusion, Jezi with skepticism. With a whirlwind of graceful drama that disrupted the entire restaurant, Morgana was gone. Keris and Jez sat at the table and looked at each other.

After a much longer lunch alone with Keris than planned, Jezi returned to the Rookery. Kass met her at the door with a cup of tea. Instantly suspicious, Jezi refused the tea and did her best to make eye contact with him, and he was being more than a little cagey. "What?" she demanded.

"Nothing, Jez. Just bringing you some tea."

"Bullshit, Kass."

"Jez, it's nothing, I swear. I did some business while you were gone. We sold something!"

Her suspicion stuttered a bit, but there had to be more to the story, or he wouldn't be nervous. "What did you sell?"

Kass had expected a different reaction. "I sold a piece of furniture, an old hutch. You know, the one with the paint peeling off and doors that looked like shutters?"

She sighed. "Kass, you make me nervous when you get twitchy like that. Selling things isn't so bad; this is a business after all." She winced inwardly and shrugged it off, with only the most minor of discomfort.

"—and a mortar and pestle set." He said it quickly, like ripping off a bandage.

Her eyes bulged, and she clenched her jaw. "You did not." Kass ducked his head. "You knew I would be angry. Why'd you sell it?"

"I don't know, Jez. She came in like she was lost, walked right to that mortar set, picked it up with big glassy eyes, and then beelined for me. It felt like one of those moments, bigger than myself."

Jezi rolled her eyes. "Kass."

"These things happen, Jez. You know that. Sometimes you have to let go. It's not like you use it anymore anyway."

She bit her tongue against everything she wanted to say. Screaming at him wouldn't change what had happened. She left abruptly. Having escaped the tongue-lashing he feared, Kass took a nap at the front desk right up to an hour before close, and then he left. When Jezi woke up the next morning, there were already customers in the shop.

It was far too early to deal with people, and Bayun felt the same way. He was sitting at the door, which Kass had apparently left unlocked, hissing at the incoming patrons. They came in anyway, unfazed. She wasn't sure what had happened, but she thought that perhaps the Rookery had been discovered, as they say. She did her best to convince them this was not a friendly shop to visit, scowling at the women and downright growling at the men. It took awhile, but the shop finally cleared out, and only three purchases happened before she got the situation under control. She closed up shop early, shooing another three people from the door who were walking up. Time to go to Morgana's.

Something was in the air; Jezi could feel it in her bones, and her bones never lied. She made her way to Morgana's house, instead of the normal restaurant. She walked up to the door, knocking lightly.

Morgana answered the door in head to toe black. She was all hair and dark lipstick, feathers and dark sparkle. Jezi was a little taken aback. Morgana had the tendency to be changeable, but this seemed new. Jezi walked in, and Morgana swept in behind her. Keris was already there, and they greeted each other wanly. The three of them made small talk awkwardly; they all knew why they were here.

"Enough of this nonsense," Jezi finally broke. "I'm not here to eat sandwiches and drink tea. I'm here to dig out the old magic." Keris tried to object and stick to her politeness, but Morgana laughed.

"I already have everything ready." She left the room with a swish of feathers and a tinkling of bells. In her absence, Jezi and Keris exchanged silent looks. This wasn't a side of her they had seen before. She wasn't gone long, and soon came swinging back into the room with an assortment of bottles, packages, and a smile. "I thought we'd start with a few potions, shake out the rust." Jezi couldn't help her excitement; there was a time when she had lived for this. Keris looked more cautious, but couldn't hide her pleasure at the sight of the collection Morgana had produced.

"The truth is I'm bored, girls." Morgana was always dramatic: flouncing, drooping, sauntering, flopping. She never just entered a room and sat down. She never simply crossed a room, or said something. If Morgana was bored, trouble was sure to follow. Keris's eyebrow arched disapprovingly. She was here, probably mostly to make sure that whatever trouble Morgana planned didn't get out of control. Morgana's plans were never small, never simple.

Keris preferred peace; Morgana thrived on chaos. Jezi didn't care what happened, as long as things didn't stay the same for too long. And things had been the same for too long. She didn't want trouble exactly, but she was interested to see what plans Morgana had in mind.

"I'm not sure, Morgana," Keris started. Morgana snuck a side-glance at Jezi and then closed her eyes and sighed.

"You never are, Keris. Come on Jez, you know a little bit of trouble is good for the soul. Stagnant water and all that. Aren't you getting a little bored in that shop of yours? Do you even sell anything in that hidden little corner?"

Jezi wasn't generally selling anything, though she hadn't made that public knowledge. The girls thought she ran that store for the money. She was getting bored though; it was time for a change.

"Wait. Look, Morgana," Keris interjected. "We all know there is no greater curse than an interesting life." Jezi smiled to herself. She had given that particular curse before, and the young man she gave it to had been so happy when he first walked out; he hadn't even known it was a curse. "Let's keep this to a minimum, can we?"

Morgana managed to look offended. "I am not trying to break anything here, Keris. I just want to have some fun. Now go get your cauldron. Don't shake out the dust; we might need that. And don't try to sneak out. We need three of us to make it work."

The night unfolded as if they had never walked away from it. The modernness fell away. Keris was Kerridwen again, in flowing white, the Keeper of the Cauldron. She was the goddess of inspiration, some said, and death in the eyes of others. Morgana was the Morrigan, the Nightmare Queen, a war goddess. And then there was Jezi. Jezibaba, or Baba Yaga in some distant past, was Crone, the Spirit of Night, the midwife of Death. There had been a time when she had been the Bone Mother. The three women stood together as though no time had passed at all.

Kerridwen's cauldron was black as night, and conveniently sized too. Gone were the days of the monstrously sized cauldrons that no one woman could lift by herself. The modern world embraced using exactly what you needed, not standing on tradition. Into the cauldron went her favorite recipe: cowslip, fluxwort, hedgeberry, vervain, mistletoe berries, and ocean foam. The last ingredient was always the hardest to obtain. Kerridwen insisted that it had to be foam from Irish beaches, which meant that shipping something that would still be fresh was the cost of the income of a small country. Jezi was simpler. She could make a potion out of anything. Snag someone's hair and whisper over it, and she could accomplish almost any goal.

Once upon a time, they would have chanted ominously while they stirred the cauldron. These days, they knew better. Intention was the key, not atmosphere. It didn't matter if you wore all black, though the Morrigan seemed to be keeping to that particular tradition. After some potion work, Keris sat down to begin cleansing as soon as she found the crystals among Morgana's stash. When she finished, she slipped a crystal into the hand of each woman.

Morgana had chosen an attraction potion and followed it by working a beautifying spell, which made both Keris and Jezi laugh.

She was always beautiful, though sometimes terrifying. Jezi chose to work jar spells, focusing her intention on protection and balance. She found a clay jar and worked mostly with herbs, though she did slip in a paper with some words written on it. When each had worked enough to loosen the kinks of disuse, they came back together to talk and discuss what would come next.

"What do you have planned, Morgana?" Keris rubbed her crystal with her thumb as they talked. Jezi's mind flitted to Kass's warning; she had chosen a protective spell for a reason after all.

"I had thought we could try a scrying?"

Jezi tried to contain her reaction. Of all she had expected, scrying was the least harm they could have done with any magic and could be useful right now too. "I have had an awful lot of business lately, so let's do it. I haven't done a scrying in many a year. When Baba's Rookery gets busy, it usually means something is going on out there. Gets the old feelings riled up, and in come pouring the heroes, just like the old days." Morgana cackled at her, but set out to clean out a glass bowl for Jezi's scrying. Keris didn't cackle; she was far too elegant for that. Jezi watched Morgana with the bowl for a second, hesitating.

"Not the glass bowl, Morgana. I prefer the old ways for this." She saw Morgana pause for a second and Keris's eyebrows furrow, but if it was going to be done it needed to be done correctly. Into the cauldron they poured a dark wine and three drops of blood, one from each woman. Together they lit three candles, one on each side.

"A black moon would have been better," Jezi grumbled, but

bent her mind to the task anyway. A witch worked with what she had. She stared into the blood red depths, watching the tiny furls of brighter red curl and wisp away, mixing slowly into the wine. Her vision blurred as she waited, but the blur materialized, and she was watching a scene. The images were unclear, and often faces were unrecognizable unless there were some other defining feature. She kept her gaze focused and waited, outwardly patient.

In the haze, she saw a raven, which wasn't too hard to figure out. She saw the storefront, the Rookery, and she saw a steady stream of people coming in and out of the front doors. This would have been more shocking had she not seen the evidence earlier that day. Then she saw him; he had the unique look of a hero. This was a hero in the old style. She wouldn't know if she was going to help him until she met him, but at least now she had time to plan a few tricks.

As the first scene faded, Yaga caught a glimpse of a face she knew well, Koschei. They had been companions now for centuries. In the beginning, she hadn't quite trusted him, keeping him at arms length, more the help than a friend. Their relationship had evolved over the years. Seeing his face now, here, she felt a pang of guilt she hadn't thought about in years. Why he would show up in her scrying, she had no idea.

She saw another face. This face was terribly old, even older than Yaga herself. Even in the old days, they hadn't had anything to do with each other. She kept herself from glancing at the Morrigan or Kerridwen. They wouldn't see the same thing as herself, and she wouldn't be able to see what they saw either. Jezi looked into the bowl again, but the face was fading, and she was already less sure about what she had seen. It had been many years since she had attempted this; perhaps she was too rusty, or overeager to see something important. In her last gaze into the cauldron, she could see nothing but stars, a broad sky studded with so many stars that they became hazy bands of milky starred blue over a pitch-black sky.

The major benefit of having the three sisters meet was this scrying. No matter how talented, one woman couldn't scry alone. But, what one woman saw was personal. Another wouldn't be able to interpret the symbols correctly, and misunderstandings could be fatal. Jezi left the gathering with disquiet in her heart. Her scrying told her that greater forces of change were at work than they had realized when Morgana had talked them into digging out the old cauldrons again. A little bit of trouble, she had said. Jezi wasn't sure what Morgana had seen, but she had left a great deal more subdued than when they showed up at her door. They all had. Yaga wanted to ask both women what they had seen in their scrying, but it was considered worse than poor manners, and they didn't offer. She tried to make eye contact with them, but the party broke up and each went home without speaking much at all.

CHAPTER TWO

"Do I remember? How could I forget?" Kass was uncharacteristically calm. "Is that what all this is about?"

Yaga nodded. "It started the night you sold my mortar and pestle." Kass broke eye contact, glancing out the formerly grimy windows to watch the passersby, who were suddenly oh-so-very-interesting. She waved his reaction away irritatedly. "Bigger than you, Kass. Don't lose focus. These things always happen for a reason. We just haven't found our reason yet." He nodded, somewhat mollified. He was dreadfully nervous around Yaga, but he had known her for a long time and had good reason to be.

He saw some of the old Yaga coming back. It had been a long time since he had seen this side of her. He could see the wildness coming out, the chaotic side of Yaga that had been suppressed for generations. Kass left her at the windows, watching for when the hero would come. He never knew, when these times came, how Yaga knew someone was coming, only that she was always ready, often with the very item in hand that they would ask her for. Each hero was different and would answer Yaga's questions differently. Kass knew there was only one way to answer her questions, and it was always the truth. Yaga could smell a lie no matter how prettily disguised it was. If someone had something to hide, they had better hide it behind truthful words, or she would find it. He had plenty of practice.

She looked less civilized as she walked back and forth from the doorway across the full length of the windows lining the storefront, a tiger pacing behind the bars of a too small cage. He felt the calmness drain away as he watched the clouds gather outside. Her wildness was calling out an answering need in himself, and he knew that if he stayed, their natures would feed off each other and create a truly vicious storm.

For this many people to visit her shop suddenly was in no way a good thing. No one visited Baba Yaga's Rookery without a purpose. They didn't always realize why they were there: sometimes it was an item, an heirloom, sometimes just words. Those words might be sage advice, or they might be a warning. Sometimes people disappeared. Not every hero deserved to complete their quest. Not every story has a happy ending, and endings were Yaga's business.

Only those pure of heart could pass Yaga's tests. A few times Yaga had to move after too many people went missing. It wasn't that she hunted people down; people came to her. All those who disappeared were spoiled in some way that she couldn't quite place. Removing them helped restore balance, and balance was what Yaga was all about: bringing down the high and mighty, bringing up the weak. Birthing babies, teaching mothers, and then helping midwife the dying again. It was all part of the cycle, each as important as the last.

In this modern world, death was a horrible, dirty secret to be hidden away. If it happened to everyone, Yaga wondered why everyone didn't talk about it, as any other experience. This modern world was strange in other ways too. People seemed to pretend that everyone was young and should stay young forever. Those who looked old were looked down on as though they had failed, made some mistake that they were paying for with wrinkles. Yaga couldn't understand it. It didn't seem that they preferred people to die young; those deaths were considered as tragic as ever – though they did tend to immortalize them. The world wanted to pretend that death didn't happen, that old age was a curse, and that women lost their value after they had their babies. Their purpose fulfilled, society didn't need them anymore, unless they planned on making more babies, but they were no longer celebrated. This culture only celebrated the young, where perfection still played in their bodies, where life had taken no toll.

Yaga preferred people who were interesting. The people she

saw all over magazine advertisements, all over television shows and movies, they were all so boringly perfect. What could possibly happen to those overly pampered pets? She preferred life, and she liked hers big. Sometimes interesting turned into mistakes, and mistakes demanded payment in many ways. But perfection, the act of life leaving no marks, took work. She wondered how long they spent grooming each morning: primping, plucking, priming, plumping. Jezi shuddered.

It seemed the greatest compliment you could pay a woman was that she looked younger than she was, no matter what age she was. Grey hair was shameful; wrinkles were something to hide or eradicate. Youth was about growth and being sharp and capable; in contrast age had become a time of decline, dull mind and lost abilities. Yaga had never been young, but each year made her sharper; she was an edged weapon, a dangerous mind. Conversely, she felt that each year brought greater contentment with her place in the world and herself as she stood in it.

Mind heavy with these thoughts, Jezi watched Kass move around the shop. He hadn't approved of Jezi getting together with the girls. "Do not trust the Morrigan," he had told her before she left. Jezi hadn't taken him seriously at the time. Morgana was one of her best and only friends, but something was in the wind — something she didn't understand. Kerridwen had been uncharacteristically quiet after the scrying, and Morgana had been impossible to read. She had no idea what either woman had seen and might never know. None of the three had offered any information, only an uncomfortable silence which spoke eloquently enough.

The next morning, Jezi was ready. She knew they were coming, so she had taken extra care of the shop the night before to make it easier for people to maneuver. She had scrubbed The Rookery down, and made it as thoroughly modern and sparkly as an antique store could be. She settled in to watch the flow of traffic. Many customers came in, and Jezi fielded them better now that she understood what was going on. A hero would be coming. She could feel herself returning to her element.

One little girl came in alone, asking for help to find a present for her mother's birthday. She already knew what she wanted and asked Jezi to help her find a momento mori ring. Jezi wasn't sure that her mother would actually want such a ring, but she didn't question it. Stranger requests had been made in the past, and often things weren't as they seemed. She happened to have such a ring in stock and sold it to the girl for three pennies and a button, which was all that the little one had in her pockets. The one who Jezi was waiting for didn't show.

Yaga turned the sign on the door as the clock hands clicked into place. The skies darkened. She had been sure that something important had been in the air, that someone would show up at the door. The clouds overhead swirled, the air began to shift and rise, and a vengeful wind tore leaves from the trees around the Rookery. Beneath the storm, a boy walked to the doorway of the shop, confused and trying to find a way in. With the shop closed for the night, the Rookery had the uncanny ability to appear as nothing but a brick wall. "Turn your back to the forest, turn your front to me," the boy called out. The store creaked, and Jezi waited. He opened the door, hesitating before he pushed it forward to walk in. He looked around the shop, not sure exactly what he was looking for.

"Jez, I've seen that boy walk by the windows several times now. Today and a few days before," Kass whispered. The boy walked directly to Yaga.

"I brought you a gift, Grandmother."

She arched an eyebrow at him and croaked a bit in response. "Yes? Not many bring me presents, child."

"I brought you something I believe you lost." He held out her mortar and pestle.

This was a most interesting development. She settled into the old patterns. "Have you anything else? This gift was already mine before someone stole it. I hope that someone was not you." Kass shifted in his seat, but remained silent.

The boy shook his young head solemnly, nervous but holding polite eye contact. "I knew it was yours. I still have a gift."

He presented her with a bouquet. Blue roses. It was an impossible thing, the type of gift few knew how to appease Yaga with. The dark clouds outside deepened. This child had to have had help. Yaga was caught between impressed and wary. Who had helped him would make a great deal of difference in how to approach this child, but she didn't have the luxury of that information.

"I thank you. What do you ask in return?"

"A question, Grandmother."

She shuddered. She didn't like questions; every question answered aged her. However, her nature compelled her to answer them with the truth. Kass, whose name used to be Koschei in the old days, chose this moment to slip out behind the shop to watch the clouds. He chuckled now that he was removed from the situation. In person, Yaga would be at her scary side soon.

"I do not like questions boy," she warned him. "I prefer to be the one asking."

"I know, Grandmother."

"Boy, are you here of your own free will, or did someone make you come?"

The boy nodded as though he had been expecting this. "I keep thinking it's because I want to be here, but when I'm not trying to be here, I end up here anyway."

Yaga nodded in acceptance of his answer. She gestured at him to indicate that it was his turn. Despite herself, she liked the boy, but now wasn't the time to show weakness. "Ask your question boy. One question. I will choose whether I answer or whether I boil your bones down for soup." The response was customary; since he was following the old rules, so would she.

The boy paled, but his resolve did not waver. He swallowed, taking a moment to compose himself. She was so proud of him, and she didn't even know him. She had to steel herself not to help him. He had to do this himself; he had to do this correctly or it wouldn't count. There hadn't been many she had wanted to help.

"You may ask me now, but remember that not every question has an answer, and not every answer leads to good. Knowing too much can make you old before your time. What knowledge do you seek from me?"

Without hesitation, despite her warning, he asked, "Grandmother, I would know how to reach the thrice nine kingdom." She blinked at him. This, she hadn't expected.

"Remember I told you that not every question leads to good? You should not ask this of me."

"This is the question I have to ask."

"Who are you, boy?"

"I am no one, Grandmother."

She didn't like him anymore. She didn't understand, but this boy could not be what he seemed.

"Ask me something else instead," she advised him, but he shook his head sadly.

"I am sorry for my question, Grandmother. I did not mean to cause you offense."

He didn't speak like a child. Where had Kass gone? Suddenly she didn't want to be alone with this strange child.

"I cannot answer that question this way. If you know to ask this question, you should know this as well." He nodded solemnly, large eyes focused on her. "Your first task is to bring me a sieve full of water."

He grinned, and the darkness lifted, the spell broken despite what had gone before. "Yes, Grandmother," he said, before he ran to the door. He pulled it open, leaning backwards to use his weight instead of his arms. He looked back at her over his shoulder before he ran out, racing the hefty weight of the door to slip out before it closed. She stared after him, trying to shake off the unsettled feeling.

Kass had been waiting outside for the weather to calm down. The clouds had swirled into interesting and confusing patterns, darkening and finally lightening. The storm began to break apart, and Kass gathered his belongings from the temporary nest — jacket, a wad of receipts, cigarettes, lighter — when the clouds darkened again threateningly. He frowned thoughtfully. There hadn't been anyone else around the shop when he left, and he didn't think a child would warrant this reaction. His naturally guilty heart skipped a beat as he walked back inside to check on Jezi, who had never once needed his help.

She was standing by the door, staring into the distance, but the boy was nowhere to be seen. She didn't look up when he entered. "Jezi?" He spoke softly, but in the silent wake of whatever had happened, it sounded like the boom of a shotgun. She didn't turn around. He didn't know what had happened, but it must have been bad.

"Jez." He touched her shoulder. She turned to see him, and her face was ancient. "What happened?"

She shook her head at him. "He asked me questions Kass, that's all." His brow wrinkled again. She waved him off. "Just one, nothing tragic. It was *What* he asked, not how many." Kass's eyebrow asked the question for him. "He asked me about the thrice nine kingdom. He came in here all frogs and snails and puppy dog tails, with those big eyes, and he asked me about the kingdom. I didn't know how to answer him on short notice, so I set him to tasks."

"Tell me you didn't give him the sieve," Kass cautioned her, knowing ahead of time that it was too late for his advice to do any good, but unable to stop himself. Kass hadn't said much before, but he had his own suspicions about the boy. He was too innocent looking, too perfectly precious. The boy had looked more like bait.

"It slipped out before I had time to think. Obviously I couldn't answer his question, and I had to say something."

He nodded at her understandingly. "It took me so by surprise. I expected him to ask me one of the impossible questions. This confirms that someone sent him to me, maybe even without his knowledge." She frowned when she said this, shaking her head, "No, not without his knowledge, but something was off. I need to talk to Kerridwen."

Morgana might be her better friend, but Kerridwen was better help in times of trouble. The Morrigan's tendency towards chaos meant that sometimes she gave answers that were more in her favor than Yaga's. Kerridwen understood the greater need and was always willing to help out in a crisis.

Kerridwen's house was the picture of perfection, complete with manicured lawn to match her manicured nails. Everything inside was precisely placed for effect. There was no such thing as laying around here. Even magazines and books were placed, never tossed. Books were not just books to read; they were as much a part of the decor as the picture on the walls. The house glowed in stark white and silvery blues, spiked with dramatically black accents. White carpet always made Yaga want to find a puddle on her way, in order to lay claim to every inch that her feet touched. Yaga's house was as opposite as possible. She wondered if a person's state of mind was evident by the state of their house. She felt that you could learn quite a bit about a person by looking at their home, mostly while they weren't there. The thought made her try to see herself through outside eyes. It also made her want to snoop around while Kerridwen wasn't watching.

Yaga had been waiting long enough to move from impatient to irritated, tapping her feet in random rhythms to keep herself occupied. Finally, Kerridwen swept into the room, two silent greyhounds shadowing her. Once she was sitting in the chair across from Yaga, she transformed the chair into a throne. Kerridwen was the Ice Queen, the two greyhounds at her side like stone sculptures, noses pointed in statuesque attention.

"So lovely for you to visit my home, Yaga. Usually we meet elsewhere. But I love it; this is an unusual surprise."

We usually meet somewhere where neither of us has the home advantage, Yaga thought, but she bit the inside of her cheek to help keep those thoughts to herself. Aloud, she merely said, "Your home becomes you, Kerridwen. Definitely a step up from the last place I saw you in." She hadn't meant to be quite so snarky, but that witch set her teeth on edge. She slapped her mental wrist, resolving to control herself.

Kerridwen's smooth brow wrinkled like the shadow of a passing storm. She chose the mostly higher road though, "I appreciate the compliment in that, Yaga. What was it you wished to discuss with me?" She then revised that slightly, to "What can I offer my help with?"

"A boy came to my shop." Yaga paused for a moment to collect herself. Her personal irritations, and the friction that arose in Kerridwen's company, had to be set aside. "I shouldn't start there. Honestly, I don't think that's where the story starts." She stopped and looked away for a moment, thinking. "While we met for lunch the other day, Kass sold my mortar and pestle." Kerridwen had the decency to look shocked instead of stifling laughter. Selling a witch's tools was no small matter. Yaga nodded at her, eyebrows high, silently reassuring her of the truth of her story.

"Yes, and since he sold them, I have had an influx of visitors to the shop every single day. Inventory — my things mind you — flying from my shelves as though there is a way to replace the preciousness of any of them."

Kerridwen thought to remind Yaga that all she had to do was close the doors of her shop, but they had been through this all before. Yaga had given up her home in the woods, but she seemed compelled to maintain a mobile location. Selling was an afterthought, simply part of the disguise that allowed her to maintain a ramshackle hut in the middle of a city.

"This isn't the part that bothered me. I wasn't sure what had been set in motion, but I knew that I would find out." Yaga paused to collect her thoughts. In her head she saw the boy and his widely innocent eyes, but she wondered if they were too blank, if his responses were not simply well-coached. "He came in and walked directly to me. Didn't waste time working up the courage to face the witch he obviously expected." Kerridwen laughed, a bell tone that grated Yaga's nerves more than it should have. She shoved her reaction back.

"He wanted to ask me a question. His responses were spot on, every time. It felt scripted. He couldn't have been sent by instinct, by an unfolding story the way the rest had. They struggle through the experience. He knew what to expect, what to say." She paused, and Kerridwen waited.

"And what did he ask you?" Kerridwen knew the type of questions that most of Yaga's visitors asked. Some came to ask her to tell their future and left more educated than anyone should be. Some came to ask for potions: to hurt those with whom they argued, to give them power where they felt weak, or to make someone fall in love. These types met with varying levels of success, based on how Yaga felt that day, as well as the truth they met her with. It had always been the same.

"He asked where the thrice nine kingdom is." Yaga stopped again and made a face. "I haven't had anyone ask that, much less a child. I didn't know how to answer him, what to say. So I sent him out on tasks."

Kerridwen took a deep breath. "Did you send him out on the sieve task?"

"Kass said the same thing." Yaga sighed. "The boy threw me off so badly, I didn't know what to say. I never send them out on the sieve task anymore. These people are too clever by far; that one never works."

"The other kingdom. We don't even talk about that among ourselves. How did he—" Kerridwen started to ask, but Yaga interrupted her.

"That's why I'm here, Kerridwen. He couldn't know; few would know, and fewer would send a child to ask me about it. Why ask me? What could someone think to achieve by this?"

"Well, don't tell him anything."

"You know it doesn't work like that. I answer questions once asked. It isn't in my power to ignore them." This was a truth that she liked to keep as quiet as possible.

Kerridwen groaned. "Put him off as long as you can. I'm guessing you already know this, and that's why you put him to tasks? And to waste one of your three tasks on that sieve? Regrettable, Yaga."

"You aren't telling me anything I don't know." She paused, uncertain whether to ask what was on her mind. "Before I go, can I ask you about the scrying, about what you saw? You were very quiet after."

Kerridwen took a deep breath. "Yaga, you know better than to ask this of me."

"I know. I know. But, under the circumstances, I just thought I'd check. Do you think it could have anything to do with all this?"

"I think," Kerridwen said hesitantly, "that you need to be careful. I don't understand what I saw, but it was Kass's face."

Jezi knew that Kerridwen had never really liked Kass, so she didn't worry too much about this. "He's harmless, I promise."

"Maybe who you need to talk to then is the Old Man." Kerridwen looked sure of herself, but Yaga was irritated. She should have thought of it on her own, but she hated visiting the

Old Man's territory. She had once lived in the thrice ninth kingdom, her hut placed on the boundary between this world and the next. Those who had traveled to see her there had already come so close and never knew.

Yaga wasted no time getting home to prepare. She sent Kass home, who was happy to oblige, and locked the door to the Rookery, something she rarely did. The easiest way to the kingdom was through her shop, the back of which was still the same hut where she had always lived. It still lay right on the border of the two worlds.

Yaga loved numbers, and she loved trying to explain their peculiar magic to anyone who would listen. Three, she would say, is a number of spirit. Things that came in threes should be paid close attention, to watch for significance, to weigh and measure in time spent thinking. Four, on the other hand, was a number of order. Things that came in fours were purposeful, more concrete, and contained less room for interpretation. If you took the perfect number of spirit and repeated it three times, you ended up with nine – three threes. It was spiritually, emotionally, psychologically perfect.

It was time for Yaga to visit the thrice ninth kingdom. She had an old man to visit. She couldn't answer the child's question, especially not without knowing who sent him. It was decided; she would leave the next day. She was waiting on Kass, who would mind the shop while she was gone. Of course she was waiting on Kass – didn't everything point back to him eventually? She felt nervous, the unplaced energy that comes before a storm. She hadn't known why, until the moment the boy walked into the shop. In his hands, he held a sieve full of water. He hadn't gone the traditional route, with lettuce leaves lining the bottom to block the holes. This child had used plastic wrap, which enhanced the effect. It wasn't leaking at all, and to the casual observer, it looked exactly like a sieve full of water. *Clever little devil*, she thought, unwillingly admiring his work. Surely someone had to be helping him.

"I completed your task, Grandmother. I believe you have two more for me before I earn my answer? I hope you will give me tasks you feel are impossible so I can truly earn it. I am excited to hear what you will have me do next." His effect of his chatter rang empty and contrived, rather than childish. It felt scripted, somehow void.

Yaga was prepared this time. She had a jar under the counter ready for this moment. She had hoped to have another day or so before he showed up with this task complete, but she had readied the jar just in case. She did not enjoy feeling that someone else was a step ahead. That was her position to hold over anyone else. This task she had never given out, so she felt it would be harder to complete. She had no doubts, none at all, that he would complete the task. Whoever was pulling his strings would be ready for the worst Yaga could give.

"You are clever, little one. Ah, and don't you smell wonderful today? I smell the spices from your mother's cooking on you, as soon as you walked in. I could bake you into a pie and eat you right up." She narrowed her eyes, sniffing, and smacked her lips. She meant to shake him up a little this time, but ended up shaken instead. He didn't smell like anything at all. No one smelled like nothing.

He didn't react much, though she thought his eyes went a little wider, if that were possible. His innocent eyes were already so big, the irises so black, that she wondered now as she looked at them. She leaned over, not quite crouching, rummaging through the cabinets beneath the register. Somewhere in this mess was the jar she was looking for. She had decided on it the night after he had come in for the first task. She had thought then that he wouldn't need much time to figure out the puzzle. This one, she hoped would take him far longer. It did depend of course, on who was helping him. She already needed to plan the next step.

She moved things more impatiently, as the jar was proving difficult to find. The boy waited patiently, watching her every move. It made her nervous, though she would never admit it. Kass walked in about the time she started slamming doors. He walked through the front door with a puzzled look on his face, already searching to find the source of all the noise in what was usually a quiet shop. When he saw the boy standing by the counter, his puzzled expression changed to one of concern.

"Jez?" From where he was, he couldn't see her. He could hear her, but he could only see the boy. "Morgana?"

"Where did you put my jar, Kass? I have been saving it, and now I need it. As in now, right now. The boy is here for it."

"Yes, I see that. I think I know where your jar is. I'll go get it, you two wait here." The boy watched him with wonder. Kass was incredibly tall, especially for an old man. Yaga looked up over the counter to see where he was going, sure that Kass had hidden it somewhere. She caught a glimpse as he was walking away that made her scowl. He was wearing pants, thank god, but underneath his vest, she saw only sagging skin. She rushed behind him to follow, partially to see his hiding place, but mostly to keep him from coming back out while the child was here. She planned to keep him from coming back to the front of the shop until he located some more clothing. To think he had been planning to come in and take over for her while she left. She growled under her breath. This time she saw a certain tightening around the edges of the eyes and mouth as he fought off the fear response.

It was comforting to her. An adult who came to her generally spent some time in fear of her, so to see a child who wasn't afraid of her was truly unsettling. Fear proved that underneath the layer of control, the child himself still existed. She had been worried that the thing in front of her was no longer a child, but an empty husk with someone else's will in control of each moment. She hobbled a bit, trying to move quickly and catch the moment Kass revealed where he hid her jar. When she walked into what passed as a storeroom, Kass was nowhere to be seen. She glanced back, unwilling to leave that child alone in the front room. Torn for no more than a few seconds of time, she turned to pass through the door when Kass came crashing back through it, jar in hand. Bayun ran out from under his feet, prompting a low uttered curse to escape from Kass's lips.

She glanced at the jar and hissed at him, "Shake that back up, you ignorant buffoon. Were you using it to practice?" He ducked his head, but his face didn't look like he felt remorse. He gave it a good shake, a roll, and a head to toe toss for good measure. She took it from him impatiently and looked it over. She could see nothing that suggested that this task could be completed easily. She shook it anyway. Cradling the jar with one crooked elbow, she turned to the front of the shop again. She hadn't turned away for half a minute, but she didn't see the boy anymore.

For a moment she felt a wave of cold heat shoot through her nervous system, a lightning shock of fear that spread from the base of her skull through her entire body. And then she saw him. He had moved away from the front counter space and was kneeling in front of a trunk of toys. The toys spilled over the top, laying around as though they had been played with and forgotten in the moment. Kass must have done that, because Yaga never took the time. Her displays were piles thrown into a corner to keep them out of the walking paths. Kass liked to make it look real.

She took the jar with her and settled again at the counter to talk to the odd boy. He pulled over a stool and jumped onto it so that he could better reach the counter to speak with her. She waited, but he didn't say anything. Clever child. Had he spoken out of turn, it would go against Yaga's rules. She did not deal with anyone who didn't speak to her with respect. In her world, children still spoke when spoken to. In her world, that still worked.

"Here is your next task." She handed the jar to him. In her hands it had looked like a normal mason jar, large enough to hold soup, which was usually why she kept them around. They often ended up collecting oddments, bits and pieces that she couldn't bring herself to throw away. This jar looked like it held dark earth. In his arms it looked massive, and he drooped under its weight.

"You will sort this jar back out to its original contents. It holds black dirt, black cinnamon, and burnt sugar. You will separate each of the ingredients into its own jar and bring them back to me."

This jar was the best of her kitchen witchery. The dirt was from the other kingdom, though she was in no way going to admit that to him. The cinnamon she had ground in her own mortar and pestle. The burnt sugar was the master stroke, in her own opinion; it looked like black earth, but made everything stick together enough to complicate an already complicated task.

He held the jar happily and shook it at eye level, watching the various ingredients shake and filter through each other as they fell. He nodded smartly and jumped off his stool. With an arm curled protectively around the jar, he ran to the door and opened it, turning back again to look at her. "Thank you, Grandmother. Is this dirt from over there? I can't wait to put my fingers into it!" And he was gone.

Jezi ground her teeth. She needed to go see the Old Man. "Kass. I have to leave. Shop is yours til I return."

He protested, "Jez, I have plans tonight."

She shook her head at him before he could finish the thought. "Nope. This has to happen, and quick."

He tilted his head at her. "Where, Jez? Where are you going?"

"The thrice nine kingdom. Tonight. As soon as I get my things together."

Now it was his turn to shake his head. "Not by yourself. Close the shop, and we'll both go. If you are going to visit who I think you are, you are taking me with you." There were times when you could argue with Kass and times when you could not. He had taken off the good natured, slightly demented mask of Kass, and he was just Koschei now. Koschei you could not fight with. Koschei always got his way. The charisma may not work on her, but this did. So she turned the sign on the glass door, turned the bolt on the lock, and they both walked to the back of the shop, through the long hallway, and into Yaga's hut.

CHAPTER THREE

The trip wasn't a long one timewise; it was long mentally. Reaching the thrice nine kingdom meant stepping sideways through worlds. Yaga had traveled to the other kingdom many times, as had Koschei. At one point, they had both lived there, on the border between that world and this. She had liked living in the borderlands, in her otherworldly hut that walked on chicken legs, spinning to avoid guests unless she chose to let them in. She had made giant shrieks, the hut would spin and creak, and she had called storms to whip the trees, break branches, and spit rain into travelers' faces. That had been in her younger days; after a while, it had all been too much work. It was easier to pretend you weren't home. No one had ever camped out on her doorstep longer than three nights. Everyone who tried to wait her out had either gotten bored, tired, or cold. A few disappeared as well, but that had been in her wilder years.

Koschei was waiting for her, but Yaga had to do a bit more preparation. The door to the thrice ninth kingdom had to be discovered, not simply opened. She had a blank wall devoted to it in her home. She gathered her ingredients, and Kass started the fire under her mini-portable cauldron—which made it so much easier to brew potions these days. To get her old cauldron boiling took a couple of hours at least, and she had to overmeasure each of a potion's ingredients to get a reasonable amount to use with that much boiling time. She had experimented with crockpots before she came up with this version. It was a small rice cooker, electric, and held just enough to make a potion for two. She threw in the ingredients, filling the container with water that she gathered only on each full moon, and kept stored in special airtight thermoses.

She had never cared for philters, although she was good with them; they were a subtle art requiring a steady hand. Herbal potions were her favorite, in the forms of decoctions and lunar infusions. She also kept many tinctures around, just in case she needed them. When the brew was done—this one was a quick design—she took three fingers and dipped them into the still-steaming, pungent water. With her wet fingers, she drew the outline of a rounded door. Once she had believed the words mattered, but she knew differently now. Still, mostly by habit, she chanted:

> Witch's potion, I enchant thee
> By intent and thrice repeated
> Be a tool of magic for me.
> Witch's potion, be now blessed
> The charm is done, the words are gone
> By the power of three by three, So mote it be.

When the shape was complete, the wall within shimmered and disappeared. She poured the remnants of the door potion into a vial which she tucked into her pocket, and then she and Kass stepped through. Doorways opened to the other side could be funny. Since the herbs were always mildly different—due to variation in soil, minerals, or rain—the doorway created was also different with each casting. Sometimes she had opened a door that she knew to be so far away that she closed it instead, choosing to start completely over. It had taken well over an hour to gather ingredients and create the potion. In the back of her head, Yaga was a little afraid that the boy would be at the door waiting, already finished with his task. She calmed the small clanging voice in her head and stepped through. Behind her, she could see the doorway framed in the air, door swinging closed, until the space through which she could see the interior of her home was just a crack. The door disappeared with the sound of air rushing to fill the void, and then it was like nothing had been there.

She was here to find the Old Man, the oldest, truth be known. She and Kass looked around, and she estimated about a half hour walk from the castle where she knew she could find him. The castle was tiny and sat dwarfed at the base of the mountains. It looked remote, with stones rippling out in three ever-widening circles. Once a traveler passed the outside circle, time began to move slower, hardly noticeable at first. The effect became more pronounced closer to the castle. When they passed the ring of the second circle, the castle was in sight, but the walk seemed to take so much longer. Each step was arduous, mind-numbingly slow, not unlike walking through water. Kass was one of the few who enjoyed the effect, and because of his peculiar place in the world, he passed through mostly unaffected. Yaga moved in slow motion beside him, which made Kass giggle almost drunkenly. The slowed effect for him was like an intoxicant.

Yaga gave up trying to carry on conversation, for two reasons. The first was Kass. Everything she said threw him into peals of drunken laughter, which took him several minutes to recover from. Since those minutes ticked by more slowly for her, the effect was torturous. The second reason was that she could feel the time stringing out between her words, and talking seemed to pull more from her. She felt it creeping up on her, aging her. She was immortal, but she didn't feel it here. Silence made it easier to bear.

They passed the inner circle, and even Kass started to slow down. His slow was far different from Yaga's, so he was amusing himself by running in circles around her. At some point, he had lost his shoes, and was pushing his bare toes through the slow rippling grass at his feet. He had unbuttoned his jacket, as well as the shirt underneath, and the folds of fabric rustled in slow motion as he moved. Yaga hated this last stretch. This wasn't the first time she had made this trip, and it hadn't gone well last time. She had been alone that time, one of the reasons she hadn't turned down Kass's support. She could see the giant double doors awaiting only their push to open, though it would still feel like hours before she and Kass touched them. Each step stretched out, and she watched that door. Even Kass's buoyant mood had turned, and he slowed beside her; together they pushed on. The process felt like nightmares where the dreamer pushes through solidified air, pulling with their arms, straining to push each foot forward, kicking and pushing for every bit of forward momentum. The closer they got to the door, the more time slowed. Yaga wasn't sure if it was worse this time, or if it was simply impossible to remember an experience like this.

Hours, days, months later, they reached the door. Kass's hands hit it a couple of moments before her own, and together they pushed, careful not to waste any movement that might distract from the purpose. Once inside, time rushed back in to fill the void, and her head felt like it might explode. She was moving too fast and too slow in the same instant. Her body felt huge in a microscopic world, and the next moment she felt as tiny as an ant, crushed under the foot of the entire universe. There was a rushing sound in her ears, pulsating, advancing and retreating; she imagined that it was her heartbeat, readjusting itself to a new concept of time.

And then it passed. There was a great stone chair in the center of the floor, flanked by two curling staircases that reached up and back to the second floor, receding into darkness. In the chair, there sat a man, beyond old. His eyes looked empty, and his face sagged with the weight of long years of experience. In the next moment, paradoxically, he was unlined and ageless, flush with sun and health. And then again, in the following moment, the old man slumped down against the stone. His eyes never left Yaga's, even as he flickered between ages. When he was old, it was as though he had always been old, and when he was young, it looked like he might never age a single day.

Yaga approached the stony throne without hesitation. She did not believe in showing weakness, and walking to this throne with anything but perfect confidence was begging for trouble. Kass took his lead from Yaga and slowed his nervous staccato walk to strolling, long strides. The man blinked at them slowly from atop his throne. The room was cold and empty. Yaga steeled her nerves and practiced her questions in her head.

"Thank you for seeing us, Father," Yaga told the man. He barely dipped his head in recognition. "I have a question I would ask of you." The man seated on the throne laughed at the irony, and the sound was the rasp of dry bones tumbled together. Even Kass shivered.

"Once again you have sought me, Yaga. Once you enter this domain, you will change. Are you prepared to cast aside what you know and learn all again?"

"Is this required of me, Father?"

"This," he rasped, a child on a throne now, "began the moment you passed the stones of the first ring."

She glanced at Kass, and he looked back at her, a pained look on his face. She shook off the feeling of subtle unrest.

"Your question, child. Ask it of me."

"A boy came to me," she began, but he interrupted her. The old man's sense of time didn't always match those who sought him, and he had his own ideas about how long a meeting should last, or how a story should be told.

"They often do, Yaga. What of this one?"

"This one, Father, he was different. I think this one has been sent. This visit was not his own decision."

"What makes you think this? More importantly, why does this bother you? Mothers have sent you their children before, often for selfish purposes, and rarely for any good."

It was true, she recognized. "Yes, but this child. I can't explain exactly why this is different. His eyes are wide and innocent; he is a pure heart, but the inside of those eyes—" she paused, looking the child over in her mind. "I think someone else is involved. Not just that someone else is guiding him. More that someone else is controlling him."

The three were silent. From somewhere in this tiny castle that seemed so cavernous, there came a tick-tock sound, both soft and booming. The man on the stone carved chair looked ancient now, older than anyone should ever be. His face was cadaverous, a skeleton stretched over with skin. The silence stretched between them, unnerving.

"Given enough time, I make all equal," he said. Yaga listened to the whispering clock in the distance and waited for him to continue, to give her something she could act on, but it seemed this was the only answer he planned to give. Regardless of who controlled the boy, for whatever purpose, the All Father believed it to be a matter in which he would not intervene. He had given her a vague warning that everything would change from this moment, and she wondered what that might mean. The clock stopped, and to all appearances, the man on the throne appeared to be lifeless. Unwilling to break the silence, Yaga and Kass backed out of the room.

Since the Old Man didn't intend to step into this conflict, it was time to call a Gathering. There were many versions of Mother Death out there, goddesses who presided over the cycle of maiden, mother, and crone. These goddesses protected the balance between life and death, and what this child was asking of Baba Yaga would break that delicate balance. A human with full knowledge of the thrice ninth kingdom would be a human who could cross over the boundary between worlds. He would effectively become immortal, outside of the system of checks and balances that restrained the hands of other immortals. Yaga couldn't let that happen.

She and Kass made the walk back from the castle. She didn't dare take the time again to walk through the stones, so she had to create a doorway within the confines of the rings. She didn't know what the consequences would be, but she didn't have enough patience to wait through the alternative. So they walked out of the kingdom using the last of the potion she had saved. Yaga didn't waste any time, but continued walking directly out the back door to the rookery that the shop was named for. She had a building out back that looked like a large dove cote. Inside, she kept exactly one hundred ravens. The ravens didn't get as much exercise as they once had, and she had finally turned the care of them over to Kass. He remembered those things so much better than she did at this point. They were excited to see her, eager and irritated at the same time. The rookery was a chaotic place, and when she stepped in she was reminded how much she loved it here.

Each bird left with a piece of paper attached to its left leg, sent them to the four corners of the earth. They would arrive in many different ways. Many of the crones were deeply inclined to the old ways, and others were more than happy to embrace the newer traditions and technologies. Once all the ravens were released, she stepped back into her workroom, where there was a circle on the ground. Inside, she closed her eyes and raised her hands above her head, palms open and outstretched.

> Maiden, spin your Circle white,
> Weave a web of shining light.
> Stag, Hawk, Bear and Wolf, Bind as one.
> Mother, spin your Circle red,
> Weave a web of glowing thread.
> Earth, Air, Fire and Water, Bind as one.
> Wise one, spin your Circle black,
> Weave the wisdom that we lack.
> Moonlight, Sunlight, Starlight, Shimmer, Bind as one.
> Lady, spin your Circle bright,
> Weave your web of dark and light.
> Earth, Air, Fire and Water, Bind as one.

The Morrigan and Kerridwen would arrive first, but it would be longer for everyone else. Most she hadn't seen in over a hundred years, although she had met each at least once. Kass was already gone for the night, so she decided to get some sleep as well. She was so tired she forgot to start a fire in the bedroom fireplace that night. The next morning, she stretched to work out the creaks as she did every morning, except that there were no creaks and no achy joints. Generally a cold sleep guaranteed a painful morning, but here she was, without carefully laid plans for pain avoidance and management, with less pain than normal mornings. She swung her feet to the edge to step down onto the floor.

Her feet felt fine; her back felt fine; her hips felt fine; her shoulders felt fine. This morning she cooked. She drank coffee, two cups, while she worked. She made eggs and bacon, biscuits and gravy. She made pancakes on a whim, telling herself that she would have guests soon to share with. She sat down to her meal, with no guests yet, and she began to eat. She ate and listened for the door, or for the ravens, and she didn't hear anything. She frowned at the fact that neither the Morrigan and Kerridwen had arrived yet. They were right here in town, no way they hadn't gotten their ravens.

She put her coffee down and stepped out back to check the rookery. She could tell by listening that some of the ravens were already back. Being her own ravens, they were preternaturally fast travelers. When she stepped inside, every single one raven had returned, and most still had the message attached to their leg. She snatched one paper from a raven leg, unrolling it to read. Her message was written inside, but had apparently never reached its audience. Just then, she heard the far sound of the front shop bell.

She felt the thrill of something akin to fear that it could be the boy. She rushed through the rooms that made up her own home, through the long passageway, and into the Rookery. Kerridwen stood just inside the door, with Kali and Santa Muerte. Of all one hundred ravens, these were the only three goddesses who had answered her call. She frowned at them. These were not the kind of women to be intimidated though, so they simply waited.

"Where is the Morrigan?"

"Jezi, you know as well as I that no one can keep up with her. I thought I would be late, so I am as shocked as you to find out she isn't here." Yaga nodded in acceptance of this.

"Santa Muerte, I am honored by your appearance. I hope you understand if we wait for the rest of our guests. I have a room in the back where we can all come together." She had met the Lady before, but had no interactions with her. Her appearance demanded a sense of formality.

The woman was tall, at least as tall as Kass. She was elegantly dressed; her hair was black as night, piled into an elaborate style studded with overblown roses and cascading curls falling to the sides of her face. The effect was beautiful, but her face was frightening. Not all goddesses could walk the world as Yaga could. Kerridwen could, though her appearance was bound to attract attention. The white of her hair and skin and the faint glowing effect combined would be hard for a person to put words to, but they would feel compelled to watch her every movement.

Lady Muerte would only be able to go public in October. She was the original Calavera Catrina, in whose likeness faces were painted into skulls and decorated with bright colors and flowers. The effect was altogether beautiful and garish and nightmarish.

The Lady's face wasn't painted to resemble a skull; it was a skull. The effect was disconcerting, hiding the ugliness of death behind the pretense of beauty and youth. Originally, it was meant to make a statement, meant to remind people of the inevitableness of death, even in the face of beauty. What Yaga was seeing in these modern days however, was that people took it seriously. The beauty was always the most important part.

The third woman was Kali. More than perhaps any other, Kali wasn't a goddess who could walk among people. She wore not a stitch of clothing, which would make Koschei proud, Yaga thought. She had four arms and pitch black skin; Kali was the black of the night sky between stars. Much like Yaga herself, Kali was not good or bad; she just was. Many of the goddesses, beyond their obvious differences, held this in common. Death wasn't a bad thing, nor a good thing for that matter; it was simply inevitable.

These women, so different from each other and yet the same, stood in the same space together for the first time. The tiny shop seemed too small, and the confines of reality were stretched taut. Yaga would have to move them to her gathering room. She walked in front to guide them through the labyrinth of the Rookery, the long passageway between shop and home, and an odd door that hadn't been there until that moment.

The room was paneled in dark wood, with an impossibly long marble table in the center. There were chairs spaced out along the table at regular intervals and bowls of fruit alternating with plates of pastries or meats spread along its length. Yaga had prepared for far more than four at this meeting. There were many Crones across the world, and she had invited every last one. The fact that only these three had shown up gnawed at the back of Yaga's mind.

They sat together at the closest end of the table. "I sent ravens to each goddess. All the ravens are home again, and almost all have the message still attached to their leg. I cannot understand why so many couldn't reach their destination." Jezi eyed the plate of pastries closest to them, but she didn't take anything. She didn't want to be the first to reach for food, and she didn't intend to deliver her information between bites. It was unlike her to be this distracted.

"Recently I started seeing people, customers, at the shop again. It started when Kass sold my mortar and pestle—" Kali and Santa Muerte both made a small horrified sound of in-taken breath at that piece of knowledge. Everyone, except for Kass himself, knew what a grave misstep that had been. He still didn't seem to get it. "Since that day, the Rookery has been overrun with customers: innocents, heroes, people who want to buy love potions, champions who want a victory potions. It's as though the gates were opened. And then there was the child. " She paused, looking at each woman, with enough sustained eye contact to ensure they would understand the importance. She still couldn't resist sneaking a glance at the pastry tray. Her stomach had the audacity to growl at that moment, and she flushed, speaking quickly to cover the sound.

"His question was about the thrice ninth kingdom. He asked me where the other kingdom was. Never in all my lifetimes have I had a human ask me that question. For him to know about it at all is already dangerous enough." The other women nodded. Yaga wasn't sure if they understood the level of danger presented, but they at least understood that this was unheard of. She couldn't stand the temptation any longer and snagged a pastry from the top of the pile. She was already licking her empty fingers before she had recognized that she was going to eat anything. The three women watched her wide eyed, but Yaga ignored them.

"Sisters, I think this is the first sign of something to come. I believe someone is controlling the child for some purpose that I don't fully understand." The other women nodded in agreement with her. Kerridwen looked away for a moment, and her normally smooth brow hinted at something that troubled her.

"Something to add, Kerridwen?" The woman shook her head, but wouldn't make eye contact. Yaga continued on, but made a mental note to speak with Kerridwen privately later.

"I have already been to talk to the All Father, and he does not wish to be involved. He seems to feel that it is none of his concern." She paused, uncomfortable. "I do not plan to leave it there."

Santa Muerte smiled at her. "I do love a woman who is not afraid to act on her own, to loose herself from the restraint of decisions that others make around her life. If you feel strongly about this matter, then you should pursue it by all means necessary."

"Lady Muerte, does that mean that you will help me if need be?" The Lady shifted uncomfortably, but could hardly do anything but pledge her help.

"What is it that you ask of me, Yaga? What do you need from

us?" she questioned.

"I fear that there is something behind the business with this child. I think it points to something else, something bigger."

"How have you put him off so far, Jezi?" this, from Kerridwen.

"I have set him to tasks. He has completed the sieve task." She held up her hand to forestall the inevitable comments. "Right now he is sorting a jar of black earth, black cinnamon, and burnt sugar." This, they approved of.

"Better start thinking of his third task now, Yaga. If he is helped, or controlled as you suspect, he will be back soon," Santa Muerte said pointedly.

"I rarely have had to give a third task, so I'm still thinking. Many of the old tasks are no longer worthy. I need it to be new, a match for a modern mind." She paused. "He will be back soon, but that's one of the reasons I wanted to meet with the other Crones. I think this is bigger than a child with questions for Baba Yaga."

Kali hadn't said anything so far, and Yaga wanted to hear what she had to say. She had watched intently, obviously following the conversation, but not offering any opinion or reaction to anything. "Kali, do you have anything, any insight for me?"

The woman was deadly even in silence. Where the other women wore the aspect of Crone, Kali was a warrior. She was Death in an entirely different form, which was, in Yaga's opinion, a fact that made her uniquely qualified to weigh in on this matter. She was a panther at rest, a weapon ready to strike. Even Yaga felt the tendrils of fear trying to worm their way into her heart, to find something to hold onto and grow from. Yaga knew how to shut it out, but no mortal would. She doubted there were many who could remain in Kali's company for long, mortal or immortal.

Despite her warrior nature, Kali was a thinker, a tactician who knew the value of a well thought out plan. "Let the boy come, Yaga. You cannot stop him, and you have already set the wheels in motion. He will not make any missteps, no easy way out for you. You already know this."

Yaga nodded discontentedly.

"The best thing you can do to prepare for your visitor is to create an absolutely impossible task. If the boy passes that test, you will know that his helper is an immortal, and then the All Father will step in."

The women all nodded, but Kali wasn't finished.

"My question though, is this." Yaga shifted her shoulders uncomfortably. "A rhetorical question then, Yaga. Why are you concerned with the boy? You have helped plenty before him, not caring why they could complete the tasks that you gave. Why the disquiet now?"

The question was reasonable. It was the same question the All Father had asked of her, but she still didn't have an answer. She felt the discomfort in her bones. Something was wrong, a fact she felt exquisitely now that her meeting summons had gone unanswered by so many. She felt sure that the two were connected, though she couldn't explain how. Perhaps it was her nature as a balance keeper. And that was it, suddenly it seemed so clear. Phrasing her response carefully, Yaga stated her position.

"I believe, Sisters, the reason for the meeting is an issue of balance. The world has moved too far to the side of youth. Old age is no longer of value and hasn't been for a long time. Age is derided, discarded, where youth is worshiped, preserved, and imitated at any cost." She looked around the table built and stocked for one hundred women.

"I don't think these Crones have chosen not to answer my call. I think these goddesses have disappeared; their places stand empty, usurped by the worship of youth." The more she talked of it, the more sure she was. "The boy is a tool, and whoever pulls his strings, that person is of interest. I feel sure that whoever this is means to take every one of us." The other women were not happy with this news, and judging from Kerridwen's face, may not even believe Yaga's declaration. Kali was nodding though. This was a war, and war was Kali's territory. She understood immediately. Santa Muerte was closer to Kerridwen's type than Kali's. Regardless, they were all in agreement with Yaga's conclusion.

"Our plan then—" Kali began, and Yaga immediately noticed the implicit we—definitely on Yaga's side then, and a strong ally. "Our plan then, is to use the boy to discover who controls him. This changes the nature of your task. It should still be unfathomably impossible, but that is only the first layer of condition. You should also think about how to create a task which will help you divine who it is that helps him. Something that will require that person leave a signature of sorts."

There it was, back to you instead of we. That's fine, she was used to it. Yaga alone. With that, she was ready to have everyone out and have her house back to herself. She would close the shop today too, sweep the cobwebs from the corners of the rooms and of her mind. Time to do some real thinking.

As the women cleared the room, Yaga snagged another pastry from the tray absentmindedly. She did her thinking better on a full belly. She wasn't sure she remembered the last time she ate this much in the space of one day. When her house was empty, she turned the sign over and locked the bolt. There was one customer she would have to deal with first. As she locked eyes with her, trying to wordlessly impress the necessity of choosing her purchases sooner rather than later, she was overcome by the thought of how old the woman was. *What an odd thought*, she mused laughingly to herself, *for Baba Yaga to think someone was old*. The old woman locked eyes with her. Yaga searched, but the woman was definitely mortal. Yaga didn't think she was here to buy anything. She was here for Baba Yaga, not antiques. Keeping eye contact, she turned the sign and the bolt. Yaga's midwife services were being asked.

Yaga worked with women their entire lives. She was there when they were born, carrying them from their mothers' wombs into the light of day. She was there when they became mothers, bringing their own children into the world for them. She was there in the twilight of their lives, helping them across the veil between worlds. In each stage, she was the midwife. Not all of those moments were pretty, but she would argue that all of those moments were positive, even in death. Death was as much a part of life as birth. She understood the grief of those left behind, but she wanted the person she was helping to understand that this was also an experience in their life, just part of the cycle. She had never understood why people were so skittish about something that happened to everyone in the human race.

The women always came to her. Yaga never sought them out. And it always ended the same. Their eyes asked the deed, rarely did they ask it with their mouths. Yaga knew how to comfort their fears, teaching them to confront those fears rather than hide from them. She knew that they needed to hear that death was not a horrible thing to spend their life fearing. She knew that they needed to hear that death wasn't the finality of everything that made them who they were. Their memory was important, the imprint of their lives onto the lives of others; the place that they occupied changed the people around them. People needed to know that in some form, they would move on to an after: that everything a person was and the things that they felt and cared for didn't end when the body died. She helped them understand that something moved on—no matter the religion, no matter their beliefs.

The old woman left the Rookery that night with her mind at peace. She left with understanding and contentment about her place in the world, in her family, and in history. She had balance, and Yaga knew exactly what she needed to do. It was strange to be suddenly in play again, when no one had sought her out in years. She was less of Yaga with each passing year, because she did nothing with the Yaga nature that was hers and hers alone. Now, acting in her capacity again, she felt stronger. The odd part was that when she looked in the mirror that night, she looked younger. It made her uncomfortable. She thought back on that morning, when her body didn't feel its customary pains. Something odd was happening, and she didn't know which of the many odd recent events to attribute it to: the boy, the potion, the doorway crossing, the stone circles, the castle, and the meeting with the All Father. There had also been the ravens, the circle of calling, the Crones, and the Crones who hadn't shown up. There had been the old woman.

It was one thing to say that balance was being disrupted, but another to experience it. Lost souls who had not found their way across the chasm between life and death clogged the street outside her shop. With the veil goddesses missing, so many had no way to find their way to an after. Yaga's appearance caused the souls outside to press forward for entrance. She pushed her way through the crowd of invisible and unhappy dead, all drawn to her because they knew that she could help. It hurt her deeply to know that they had been left on their own in this way. Though it was very late, she held the doors open, and the souls flooded through.

Not all spirits got lost. Some souls become disoriented, unable to cross without assistance. Not everyone could die in peace, and those unhappy souls needed the midwife's help. She would calm them, help the body release the soul, and then help that soul make its way through the door, or the stairway, or whatever appeared to them personally. Some needed more help than others. With no Crone available but herself, the veil would be thick with lost souls. She wondered how many the veil could hold before it ruptured, spilling them back onto this side to wander lost in their own last moments.

Yaga stayed up for three nights helping each souls across. The state of balance couldn't be ignored, and since she was the only one left, the task would fall to Yaga. The words of the All Father's warning looped back to her: "Once you enter this domain, you will change. Are you prepared to cast aside what you know and learn all again?" To learn all again. She wasn't sure if it was a reward, a promise, or a threat.

A younger Yaga when all of creation was out of balance, with the boundary between life and death weakening, was not a strength. Young Baba Yaga was a thing that should not be. With someone culling the goddesses who presided over death and balance, she needed all of her wisdom and sharpness. Then it struck her; this was a good thing. This youth she had been given removed her from the dangerous identity of Crone. Perhaps the All Father had intervened after all. She would age backwards because of her trip through the stones. They had cast the doorway inside, and so had never walked back through the stones; the aging process had only gone in one direction. She needed to see if Kass was under the same reversal effect as she was experiencing. He wouldn't be in until the following day. She would have to wait.

Before bed she ate another huge meal, mostly meat, and washed it all down with beer and milk. She didn't light any fires, and Bayun stayed a semi-respectful distance away, blinking at her in the way that cats have. He winked at her, one eye at a time, in something like ancient Morse Code. Indecipherable. As she drifted to sleep, she felt she would understand the universe if she could decipher the language of cats.

The next morning, she woke and felt fifty. Being a Crone, having always been a Crone, Yaga had never been fifty years old. It felt like springtime; she didn't know how young people could stand the feeling of movement in their very bones, driving them to be up and moving, to be active and participate and belong and respond and talk and eat. Her body was aging backwards, younger and younger now, and she was intoxicated with it. The food was glorious; everything was glorious. Yaga caught herself dancing. She finished her shower and looked at herself in the mirror, hair loose and wet over her shoulders. Even as a Crone, Yaga always wore her hair long. Generally it was thick and wiry, iron grey. Now it was chestnut brown, soft and wavy. She was shocked when she looked at her own face. Everything was softer. The skin around her eyes had lifted, tightened. Her face felt more relaxed and looked brighter. Her skin was soft and glowing, more like Kerridwen's than her own.

She looked thirty: vibrant, healthy. It was exhilarating, although she also felt a vague sense of shame. She had never understood the desire to hold onto youth. She had always been proud of her age, of her nature as a Crone. With youth clinging to her, she felt the tug now that she had never understood before: the fear of its loss.

Over the next few days, the atmosphere of the Rookery changed. Yaga kept finding people who needed help: people hurt in body, people hurt in soul. Everyone needed a different kind of help, and Yaga felt compelled to help them all. This was the voice of Raven, the voice she had suppressed for years. Raven had always been Yaga's speaker, but she had been hiding, pretending she was mortal for generations now. Yaga had been hiding from herself, and her story had diminished over time.

She had gotten tired of helping, of hurting, and had chosen to fade into the woodwork. She was tired of being seen only as a witch, as a negative power, when she knew how much good she had once done in the world. It wasn't that she didn't do bad things too, but everything Yaga did was in balance. It was bigger than herself. If something bad happened, something good had to happen to balance it.

It was into this state of affairs that the boy walked back into the Rookery. Yaga was at the counter when he walked in, where she had been talking to the customers. They treated her differently now; they were friendly. She commanded fear and respect as Yaga, but as her younger self she gained friendship and camaraderie. People enjoyed her company. Yaga wasn't used to people wanting to share her time, so she reveled in it.

No one else had walked in and recognized her, but the boy walked in, looked around, and walked straight to Yaga with no hesitation. "Grandmother," he started, and she spun around, startled.

"Grandmother?" she questioned, incredulous that he still knew her. This child, he got under her skin.

He nodded. "Of course." He saw her; he saw Yaga, not her skin or her hair or her wrinkles.

"Who are you, boy?"

"I am no one, Grandmother. I seek answers only."

"Who do you seek these answers for?"

"For myself, Grandmother."

She shook her head. "There is someone else, someone who helps you. There always is. No child has ever passed the questions and the trials without help."

"That's why I'm here though, Grandmother. The second trial, I can't figure it out. I wanted to know if there was a key of some kind, something that you do to help me."

She blinked at him. This was not the direction she had anticipated. She fully expected him to show up with three tiny jars, each perfectly sorted into dirt, sugar, and cinnamon. He held out his two hands, a jar. Her jar. She looked at it, and she looked at him.

"I do not help. I am the doorway; I am the gatekeeper. I give the impossible tasks." This speech wasn't making her feel stronger. She felt petulant. She decided to stop talking. He didn't say anything; he watched her. His eyes were so innocent. He held out the jar again. He shook the jar again slightly, and the colors shifted slightly. She tried to keep her eyes on his. He shook the jar again, ever so slightly. There was something menacing in the blank innocence of his wide eyes. The contents of the jar were sifting as he shook the jar. She could see the impossible happening. Every slight movement he gave the jar—and he was so calculated—settled the contents ever so much. He gave it one final shake, and the layers were complete. A stripe of black cinnamon at the top, a stripe of burnt sugar in the center, and a final stripe of black earth along the bottom. She met his eyes, and they were hard. Her eyes were harder.

The whole exchange was staged: the innocent eyes, the pleading request, the final conquest. And now he was going to ask her for a final task. She wasn't ready — then, a stroke of brilliance. What was the one thing that the boy, or better yet, that the puppet master did not want to do?

"Your final task is to tell me your name." The boy opened his mouth to answer, too quickly, and she stopped him with an outstretched hand. A beautiful hand with smooth skin and plump fingers. "Not the boy's name. I'm not actually talking to him though am I? I want your name. I want to know who I'm talking to. Come here, come meet me in person, face to face."

The boy wasn't talking, and she thought she could feel the eyes behind his own eyes.

"Release the boy. Why hide behind a child? Come and confront me yourself."

And then he spoke. "There is no one but myself. I am the one who speaks." She looked in his eyes again. She looked with Yaga eyes, the eyes that could seek truth, and she saw all she had ever seen. She saw the boy. She saw deep eyes, but there was no one behind them. What she was seeing was incalculable depth. She was seeing immortal. Who was this child, and why had she rattled off a task without thinking about it longer?

He spoke with another voice, one without gender, multi-layered as though many spoke at once. "While you have wasted your time here in your little hut, while you have worried so much about the boy, I have taken them all. I have tracked down every single one of those who guard death's door. I have shown them across that portal for themselves." Yaga couldn't tell anything about the speaker, but it made no difference. The entire ordeal had been staged to keep her busy. No matter who it was, she would find them.

With that the boy dropped dead. With the power controlling him gone, the boy looked hollow and neglected. The illusion of health faded, and Yaga was shocked at the state of his body, that he had still been alive at all. She needed to find who was behind this disgusting parody of innocence. The dead child at her feet demanded her attention. For his sake, whoever he had been before, she had to attend to him before she could do anything else. She hated that his life had been stolen from him, in so many different ways. She hated that he had been made to face this kind of death, a death that instilled fear. Before she even knew who it was, she hated whoever was responsible. Yaga had never hated anyone; she was balance, understanding the necessity of evil in the world. A passionate nature ran high in this youthful body, and she felt herself burn with rage.

She took the body with her, gathering him gently to her chest as a mother would a child. He weighed hardly anything, and she wondered if he had even been alive, or existing in a reanimated state. This boy had likely been chosen as one who wouldn't be missed, though it hurt her heart to think it. She washed him, and she wrapped him in the style of the Old World. When she had finished she knew but one thing. It was time for the hunt.

Baba Yaga walked to the door with hard eyes, ready now for

the confrontation she had been avoiding. She grabbed her broom from the corner, her most precious possession, the old silver birch broom that she never used for sweeping. Yaga could use this broom to sweep behind her to erase any trace of where she had been. She had a task, but she had no idea who could be behind this awful distortion or what the point had been. She was going to find out.

CHAPTER FOUR

The All Father did not belong to any one country or culture. Everyone called him something different, but names didn't mean anything to him. There were not multiple versions of himself around the world, all performing a similar role. There was only himself. He was outside the petty affairs of mortals, even of immortals. Eventually, everything came back to him in some form. The Father of All was known by many names, but modern mortals might recognize him as Father Time: reborn each year as a tiny babe, a dying god at the end. The king is dead; long live the king.

Yaga wasn't sure why she had been given the gift of youth; she had never been anything but a Crone. She was spectacularly well suited to the job requirements. The timing of this gift, which had to have been the doing of the All Father, had to be important. He had known what was happening, though he had chosen not to get involved. He always did know. It was an irritating constant in all of their lives. So, it only made sense that the All Father had known all of these pieces, and more, that Yaga had only begun to put together.

She was tempted to go back and to seek his input with the new developments in mind. She stopped herself though; he had made his position clear. He didn't wish to be involved in the matter, for reasons known only to himself. She didn't think he would change his mind on this, so as much as she wanted to go back to see him, to seek out the easy answers, it wasn't going to work. She would have to figure this out, and what to do next, on her own. What Yaga needed to do was clear her head. The need for retribution felt physical, clouding her sense of reason, slowing her thinking. It was as though her mind was sharper in a body clouded by age, and this young body whose muscles responded with clarity was clouding her mind. She snatched up her broom to go for a walk, trusting the wind to take her where she needed to be. Kass met her at the door. He stopped short, staring at her. She snapped at him before she realized why he was so confused. Kass hadn't seen her yesterday.

"Jez?" He cocked his head to the side, the matching tilt of his eyebrows betraying his confusion. He always managed to come in at the wrong time. She had already moved past this, and was ready to leave, to clear her head and fix what she felt was her responsibility in the boy's death.

"Yes, Kass. Come with me, and I'll explain." She dragged him out the door with her, and locked it behind them. She unlocked it again, stepped inside to flip the sign over to tell people that the shop was closed, and then ducked back out to stand by Kass. Once the door was locked, she took Kass's arm conspiratorially. She half dragged him along with her, more intent on what she wanted to tell him than on the polite level of her words or actions. She knew he was still looking at her strangely, but she didn't have time for that.

"You have been missing a few days, Kass." She glanced at him from the side as they walked. For some reason she didn't want to stand talking; she felt urged to movement.

He ducked his head a bit. "Are you kidding, Jez? Have you seen me? I had to get out there and make some friends while this lasts."

What she felt was something between irritation and amusement, and she couldn't help but chuckle. As soon as it occurred to her, once she had moved past the awe of her own youth, she had known exactly where Kass was. He was still an ugly bastard, but as always, he had a certain charm. He was tall and spindly, but on the younger body his wild hair was rakish and disheveled, where it had looked like seaweed when he was old. He wore jeans, and being so skinny, he wore them loosely. He had on a black jacket and clunky black shoes. She imagined that girls who went for the professor look were all over him. *He did love to tell stories*, she thought ironically, laughing to herself. She hadn't planned on taking this younger body out, but she was feeling the temptation. More than she had expected at first. She pushed it back again. She had work to attend to, and it was Yaga work.

"Kass, I have—" she paused, thinking, "an awful lot to talk about with you." She didn't know where to start. What was more important? "The boy. He came back. It was so strange though, he was almost threatening." Kass didn't laugh at the image; he had also seen the strangeness around the boy. He knew that unnatural solemnness as well as she did. "Someone else spoke through him, and he completed the sorting task in front of my eyes. He brought the jar back, to ask for my help in sorting it," she shook her head at that again. "And then, something changed. His eyes were hard, and it was someone else—looking through him."

She shuddered and looked at Kass. He was watching her. "What happened, Jez?" His face mirrored her own guilt and sorrow.

"Whoever it was, they killed him. He shook the jar until the layers sorted themselves out. A human can't do that. And those eyes. It wasn't him anymore. And then, as though someone flipped a switch, and he was gone." She didn't say how awful she had felt. Kass knew her well enough, he would know how hollow she felt at this type of death, especially for someone so young. Torn out of life, violently removed from his natural pattern. This was the type of death that was likely to create trouble in the scheme of balance.

"On top of this, Kass, there is the matter of the Crones. I called a meeting before the boy even came back. When we got back from the stone rings, I knew something big was afoot, and I felt that there needed to be more who could help address it." She had been upset that the All Father was not going to step in. She had known then that it was an immortal issue, politics. She couldn't believe that the All Father hadn't stepped in on the issue, or what might still be at stake.

"Only three of them showed up. The rest, the messages didn't go anywhere. The ravens were all back by morning, and all the messages were still intact."

"Who showed up?"

"Kali and Santa Muerte, who I've never had much contact with. Kerridwen of course, but not the Morrigan. She's going to be the first one I try to go find. I must know what's happening." Kali always showed up when there was chaos in the air, but The Lady had always stayed to herself. Her presence in the absence of the others was a matter of concern in itself.

Kass's face still echoed the self-reproach Yaga felt over what happened with the boy. "I'm sure Morgana is fine. You know how she is." He shrugged, looking uncomfortable. "I'll do some looking around as well, Jezi, see what I can do to make this right." He would too, she knew, but in his way, and in his own time. His methods didn't usually make much sense to Yaga, and she knew better than to rely on him much for anything.

Her first step was the Morrigan. She was going to go find her and see what was going on. Kerridwen hadn't known anything then, but maybe she had heard something since. Yaga traveled to the Morrigan's house first. It was a big house, empty and dark. There was no one home, and no sign that anyone had been there for some time. She went to Kerridwen's house next, irritated that she had to call first in order to gain entry past the gate. The lake was troubled by autumn winds, and leaves tumbled in the streets monotonously. This was usually Yaga's favorite time of year, but now everything grated on her nerves.

Kerridwen's house was pristine as always, white and shining, but she wasn't there. Her husband seemed distracted, but didn't offer any further information. Yaga had never been one of his favorite people to deal with, but he simply did not recognize her. No doubt he thought she was one of the countless women who sought out Kerridwen's help. She let it go. It would be too complicated, too drawn out, and likely the man wouldn't care what her story held. She left with no better information; except that now she knew of one more goddess who was missing.

Yaga burst into the shop, but Kass wasn't there. The door was open, and there were two or three customers wandering around, picking up objects reverently and turning them over in eager, but careful, hands. She checked every room of the tiny labyrinth of a shop, but he was nowhere to be found. She growled to herself, but shelved the reaction for the moment and helped the customers first. The first customer had stumbled into the shop while walking in the neighborhood, and didn't need any help thank you, but it was a great little shop. Adorable. Yaga nodded politely and went to help the next customer. The second patron had heard about the Rookery from her daughter and was coming to search through what an amazing historical treasure trove she had heard about. She looked mildly disappointed, but determined to find those seriously special items, wherever they were hidden. Yaga left her to her mission, focusing her attention on the final customer, who had wandered into one of the side rooms.

She helped the first person find something he hadn't even known he was looking for, and he left delighted. The second customer left happy as well, she felt positive that she had found a better treasure than her daughter had, and couldn't wait to go show it off. Yaga laughed to herself, because she had seen how many truly wonderful items the woman had passed up to choose the little book she had finally left with. Two books away on the shelf was a signed copy, first edition of a significant book that would have made the woman semi-famous. Well, the type of famous that would last a couple of months, at any rate. There was a final customer who didn't look lost; he appeared to be waiting. He wandered through the rooms aimlessly, looking at the antiques with no real interest. Yaga understood that this wasn't an antiques patron, this person was waiting for Baba Yaga.

The last customer made his way to Yaga after the shop was empty of anyone else. "I hear you have other things that you sell, not antiques I mean," he stammered. She didn't answer him, as he had not phrased a question to her. He fidgeted, but held his resolve. "A dark lady of magic, I mean. I am here to ask for something from you." Again, she simply waited, as no question had yet been posed. She watched him mildly, offered a blank expression. "I seek a wife," he pleaded finally. She breathed in and closed her eyes to control her desire to snap at the man.

"There are other ways," she told him.

"Not for me," he replied softly. He was a man of modest means, of modest looks, and modest demeanor. But none of this meant he could not have a wife. She softened, but only a bit.

"You should go bake bread for her," she told him.

He nodded eagerly. "Yes, I've read of this - three loaves."

"No, just go bake bread."

"And you have a magic ingredient for me," he anticipated.

"No, just go bake bread."

He looked at her warily. "But, aren't you — "

She interrupted him before he could ask a question. "It doesn't matter. Go do what I've told you. Go share your bread with this woman. You have already chosen one, haven't you?" He nodded to her, somewhat unhappily. "You will see." Not every task had to be completed with magic.

With the shop finally closed for the night, Yaga had other work to complete. Unlike the stories about witches, Yaga's broom wasn't how she traveled. Her mortar and pestle were for travel, paddling through the air with the pestle as an oar. It was a diabolical piece of magic, and Kass had always hated it. When not in magical use, it appeared to be used to crush herbs. When she wanted to travel, it was the size of a small boat. She was going to use the mortar and pestle to travel to check on the other missing goddesses, and the broom was more of a tool. The broom she used to sweep her trail behind her so that no one would be able to see her or to track her as she traveled. Whoever was behind the crones who had gone missing, she didn't want to attract their attention. She wanted to be the one who struck first. Yaga didn't like to be the one surprised, but she did so love to be the nasty surprise.

Her first stop was in India, to make sure Kali was okay. Kali was, of course, but she was in no mood to be social. Yaga checked in long enough to make sure she was okay and took off again. She travel to each country, checking in on goddesses of every heritage. Russia, Greece, Brazil, Japan, and Mexico, all missing. If she and Kali were the only goddesses left, the only ones holding the balance between life and death, the boundaries between the natural transitions of life would start getting more fluid. There would be problems with aging, with delays in death. That line of thought led back to herself and Kass and the reverse aging they had both experienced. She had chalked it up to the stone circles, but now she wondered.

If all the immortals who so carefully protected that boundary disappeared, the veil would weaken. This aging problem could simply be a sign of that weakness. She was already headed home, and she needed to go find a mirror, to examine the evidence for herself. This could be more of a curse, if the aging reversal was still ongoing. She had thought it would be a temporary effect from visiting the All Father, but it wasn't the first time she had gone. She had simply chalked the difference up to the effect of multiple visits, or the placement of the return doorway.

She only knew of Kali still out there, and she wasn't sure anyone could overpower Kali. No other goddess was such a warrior as she. But, if Kali were to disappear as well, that would only leave Yaga. Soon, if not already, whoever this was would be coming for her. She couldn't imagine what their goal might be.

What could someone possibly gain by removing the threshold between stages of life, including death. Yaga's thoughts drifted as she lay unsleeping in her bed that night. Who stood to gain from this? All signs so far pointed to Yaga herself. She had gained so much power from this process, and she hadn't even realized what was going on. She wondered how this was affecting the process of death. Would there still be death without the goddesses who tended the veil? She felt sure that there would be. Death wore many faces, and Baba Yaga had many names.

She fell asleep with her mind moving a hundred miles a minute, and her dreams were vivid and uncomfortable. She dreamed of a coyote chasing the sun and moon round and around the earth after releasing them from a box that was far too small to have contained either. The people of light, they had called themselves. The dream shifted, and she dreamed of a box again, and a girl who had opened the box, only to release the most horrible things from it. They had swirled around her, and the dream shifted into a nightmare, because one of the horrible things wore Baba Yaga's own face.

When she awoke, she felt different. She rushed to her mirror to check, and the face that met her own was plump and rosy. It would have made her laugh, but mostly it frightened her. Yaga wasn't used to being frightened. In her own kitchen, puttering around to make what was now her customary breakfast, she found her poppy seeds. She was going to make poppy seed pastries, until she opened the container and found that most of the poppy seeds had turned to dust; but that was impossible. She hadn't opened the container for some time, but she knew poppy seeds would not turn. She wondered if it was Kass trying to be funny again, and then a shiver ran up her spine. This wasn't a joke, this was a message. Poppy seeds were part of one of Yaga's spells for sleep, but could also be used in a spell to bring on death, or the long sleep. She felt certain that the dust of the decayed seeds was meant to tell her that her own death was approaching. Who was powerful enough, or stupid enough, to challenge Baba Yaga? Few were in a position to try.

She thought again of all the missing goddesses, and her blood ran cold. If Kali was the only one left, that could only mean one thing. Kali had to be behind the whole mess. Maybe she had found a way to kill off the other Crones, to gather their power to herself. The Mother of Chaos would love nothing more than to be the most powerful in the world. Yaga wondered if she hadn't looked a bit younger after all, when she had gone to see her last. She had chosen not to interrupt her because Kali was always wrapped up in business, and business was usually bloody. It was time to go talk to her, find out what was going on, and a way to bring back the other goddesses. You could neither create nor destroy an immortal, they say. She meant to find out.

She grabbed her broom and jumped inside the mortar to make her way back to India. Yaga didn't care what Kali was doing when she showed up; they were going to talk. The trip was ridiculously fast, as all magic trips should be. The grounds looked just as they had the day before, except that now the lights were on in every room, and loud music was streaming from the windows.

Yaga strode into the house fiercely, swinging her head around to see the first sign of the chaos goddess, but there was no one to be seen. A tortured scream echoed through the empty halls. It was deafening, even louder than the music in the house. She rushed the stairs, intending to save whoever was being brutalized by a woman notorious for torture.

The only living soul she could see was a tiny girl, black skinned and black haired, curled up in the center of the bed screaming. This must have been who she had heard. Peeking at Yaga from under protectively crossed arms, the girl wrapped them around her knees for an extra barrier. Yaga approached her slowly. "Where is Kali," she asked.

"I am Kali," came the answer. Yaga was stunned. Even as she turned this revelation over in her head, the girl screamed again, and her flesh began to darken and crumble. It was agonizingly slow to watch; the girl's screams went silent as her throat turned as well. Her face was last, and she locked eyes with Yaga right before she was gone. There was the shape of a girl lying on the bed now, curled into a fetal position in the center of the bed.

As Yaga watched, the girl shape dissolved into a pile of earth. It looked like the earth in her jar: black earth from the Motherland. She watched Kali, who had reverse aged so much that she was a child, and she knew that all the others must have gone the same way. Yaga felt her heart would fall apart as well.

She sat alone in an empty room, wondering if she was the last. She felt numb and wasn't at all sure how to handle what she had witnessed. *Could immortals die?* She didn't go home, half afraid Kass would be gone, half afraid he wouldn't. She took her time, but there was nowhere else to go. Her mind raced. With Kali's death she had felt a rush of uncomfortable power that told her that whatever Kali had lost, she had gained, at least in part. Someone had to be masterminding this, trying to bring together what power each of these goddesses had been forced to leave behind.

When she arrived home, the front shop looked like it had been robbed. Every precious thing had been broken, the more everyday items tossed around. Every light in the room was on, and Kass was naked in the center of the room. She couldn't tell if Kass was a victim or the culprit. The bell rang out when she opened the door, and he looked up drunkenly.

"What happened?" she wailed, holding her hands out, palms up, as if to hold all the broken things, to show him what he apparently wasn't seeing.

"Someone—" he slurred, "someone came looking for you. I knew you said you thought there was someone out there with bad intentions, so I didn't wait to see who it was. I took a swing."

"But," she stopped and blinked at him. "Are you drunk? Why is the shop trashed? For Goddess' sake, why are you naked?"

"Well, we had a drink together first," he defended.

She boggled at him. "You and who?"

"It was Morgana. She stopped by looking for you."

"Oh, Kass."

"Now, Jez, it wasn't like that."

She shook her head at him. "I don't even know what to say. How did this happen? You'd better start at the beginning, and please, please—put some clothes back on before you do anything else." Koschei never did have a sense of shame, not then, and not now. He did, however, know when Yaga was serious. He stood up, fully unselfconscious, and walked to the back of the shop where he had apparently vigorously removed his clothes. They were strewn everywhere. Pants were hanging over the counter; shirt was draped haphazardly over a chair. There were socks and underwear thrown to the side, landed against the door to her own rooms. At least that door was closed.

She tried not to watch as he retrieved all his various accoutrements, half because she didn't want to encourage him. She could see him from the corner of her eye, smirking at her. He was incorrigible. "You may as well start talking, Kass. Tell me from the beginning."

He stopped in mid pants arrangement, apparently unable to think and follow simple instructions at the same time. She grimaced when she saw him grin at her. *Foolish thing*, she thought, not entirely sure if she meant him or herself.

"I told you I would poke around, see what shook loose. Well, Morgana showed up, and everything was fine at first. She asked where you were, and since I didn't know, I didn't tell her." He paused, adjusting his zipper, and slipped the shirt over his head. "Everything was fine at first; she had brought a fancy bottle, and you know I can't resist those amazing Russian spirits. So we drank, and we talked. She was more than happy to keep my glass topped up. She didn't seem to be leaving any time soon, and she definitely wasn't drinking as much as she was offering. Things didn't get weird until I told her that you were looking for the other Crones and Veil Mothers."

Yaga waited. Sometimes the best path to truth was silence.

Kass shook his head like he was arguing with himself. "When I talked about where you were and why, she seemed angry. She didn't say anything to make me think this, mind. It was that I saw a difference in how she acted, how she talked. Where she had been friendly, now she was irritable. She poured me another drink, a bigger one. She was more aggressive, and I felt a fight in the air. You know I fight better with my clothes off, so I slipped off my shoes, casual-like. I could tell something had changed, and the Morrigan is not a girl to be messed with—I should know."

Yaga nodded at that. Whatever had set her off, the Morrigan could be dangerous once roused from her content state.

"She saw me slip my shoes off I think, and it made her suspicious. She asked me to go get her something ... and I can't even remember now, because when I got back, she had poured me a new drink, and after that one, I hit the floor." He looked around as though only now seeing the damage. "Did I do it, or did she?"

"I'm guessing that she did, or that someone broke in after you crashed out. You must be forgetting something important though, because you aren't wearing a stitch of clothing. It wasn't just your shoes that you took off."

"I think there was something else in that drink. She must have slipped something into it. After that last one, I don't remember much. Everything went big and loud, then hazy, and then nothing. Just black."

Yaga had seen him after a blackout drunk before, and it took a lot, but she had also seen him go into a black rage. This could have gone either way.

"Jez, I did notice something before I blacked out. She looked younger. I mean, Morgana has always had that effect, but she definitely looked younger. It must not have been the stone rings, or the All Father, who did this to us." Yaga smiled at that one. Kass was quick, but he would never be as clever as Yaga. Not by half.

"Kass, I want you to stay with me for this next part of my journey. What I feel in the air is change. I have been out afar tonight, and I have hunted down each and every goddess that I know. They are all gone. When I leave again, I will hunt one whom I have never spoken with before. She is not from our realm exactly, but I think she will be of assistance." She paused and made eye contact with him. "And I do not want you here alone." There was something more to this story. Kass's account of the events didn't quite add up.

He tried to protest, but Yaga wasn't hearing it. Whatever had happened here last night, she did not want him here alone for what came next. If Morgana had been looking for her, she would be looking for answers as well. Someone had to know what was going on. In the old days, they would consult the Oracle, but Yaga had bigger plans. Yaga was going to go see Oya, the one who sees and hears all. If anyone had their eye on changes in the wind, it was she.

"Let's eat breakfast before we go, Kass. I'll cook for you." Kass looked at her suspiciously. Poor thing, he might never recover from the indignity of someone spiking his drink. Yaga couldn't understand why she was always hungry now, but wondered if it was something to do with the aging. Her body was trying to eat enough to cover the ferocity of change that she was undergoing. Kass followed her back to the kitchen. She looked at him playfully and broke an egg into the skillet. Kass had a interesting history with eggs, and she loved to harass him with it: a long standing joke between them that was only funny to Jez.

"Eggs for you, Kass?" He pretended not to care, shrugging a shoulder at her.

"Only if you fry them. I hate them scrambled."

"I have a big treat for you this morning. I brought duck eggs back with me, so we will feast as we did in the old world this morning."

He shuddered and put his hands up. "None for me thanks."

"No? I found these special." She cracked another egg at him ominously, watching him wince as she brought the shell down smartly on the metal edge of the skillet.

"Just coffee, Jez. I've lost my appetite."

She chuckled to herself and swished all the eggs together into a big scrambled mass, adding a bit of milk and cheese and letting them bubble in the big flat skillet. She sprinkled on onions and crumbled bacon, fresh chopped chives, and folded it all over to seal it. She ate the whole thing by herself, and chased it with two cups of black coffee. Kass watched her over the edge of his cup.

"What's got into you?" He looked uncomfortable, he hadn't eaten anything at all, and despite her jokes, she didn't think it was about the egg. The appetite might not be about the aging, because he did not seem to share her ferocious need for food.

"I'm just hungry, Kass. It's intense, it feels like if I don't eat right then and keep on eating—" she broke off, uncomfortable. "I don't know. It feels like the tide pulling on my blood, almost irresistible. Animal." She hadn't tried to explain this yet, and it was harder than she expected. It wasn't just hunger; she was insatiable. "None of this is important though. Listen, here is my plan. We need to go see Oya. The Mother of Nine."

Kass kept shaking his head. It didn't seem to matter what she said today, Kass didn't want to hear it. "You keep talking nonsense, Jezi. What could you possibly need of her?"

"Oya Yansa, she's the one I need. She is the goddess of change. This is a time of change, so if anyone can help us understand what is going on, it will be her."

That made sense, but he still didn't like it. Oya, who went by many names, was more warrior than goddess, much like Kali. She was unpredictable, and Kass didn't mind admitting it, downright scary. She tended to scream randomly, and it didn't take long for that kind of behavior to unsettle a man, no matter how powerful he was. She sounded like a Banshee, she did. He was already uncomfortable thinking about her.

Against his wishes breakfast was over, and they were flying in Yaga's mortar and pestle. It hadn't been a genuine accident that he had sold the thing. He hated it. He hated its impossible nature, and above all he hated flying in it. He thought it was stupid. And it was scary. Who flew in a thing that could dump you out like a boat if you got too curious and tried looking too far over the edge? Yaga ignored him and steered them across the sky using the pestle as a rudder.

Yaga took them right to the edge of a cemetery, where she knew that Oya could be found. They could already hear her; over the sound of the wild winds that always followed that woman, she was screaming. It couldn't be a good thing for two goddesses and Koschei to meet up in one location, all of whom had an effect on the weather. They would have to make their business quick before they created a superstorm. Yaga was more worried about the source of the screaming, since she had so recently been to visit Kali and seen the results of whatever had happened there.

Oya Yansa was the guardian of the underworld, as well as a force of destruction in the form of hurricanes and tornadoes. She was akin to the Crones but also a goddess of magic and fertility: a giver of life. She wore cloth made of fire, of every color except black, burning but never burned. Yaga and Koschei stood at the gate to the cemetery, waiting for the elusive woman, whom Kass insisted that he didn't really want to find. Yaga shushed him. With both Yaga and Koschei standing there, the clouds were already starting to darken and roll ominously. Adding one more weather-prone immortal could make this night become too interesting by far.

Yaga waited at the gate, and Kass watched the clouds. They both knew when she was coming, and she had undoubtedly known they were there from the moment they arrived. The waiting time between then and now was all strategy. It wasn't the clouds; they knew Oya was coming because they could hear her screaming. It was eerie and frightening, even to immortal ears, and Yaga could only imagine how a human would react to an encounter with the Mother of Nine.

The screaming continued once they could see her. She walked through the cemetery, angling between graves respectfully and touching headstones as she passed. She walked right up to the gate, where Yaga and Kass had stopped to ask before they attempted to gain admittance. The screaming continued, right up until Oya stopped walking, waiting in front of them at the gate. The boundary stood directly between them, and Oya stood in the center, feet planted wide as though she would bar entry. Though Oya was a slight little thing, Yaga knew that she could keep them from coming through the gate unless she wished it. Oya Yansa's reasons were her own; while a hero might gain entry on one occasion, that same person might be denied the next and could be killed for asking on the third. Her reasons were inscrutable. In her head, though never aloud, Yaga thought of Oya like the Sphinx: a certain feline quality here and a matching feminine quality there. The Mother of Nine wasn't far from being related to the Sphinx; both were fierce guardians, both fond of riddles.

The woman before her was draped in a floor length cloth gown that shimmered with rainbows and broke out into little fires all up and down its length.

"Yaga."

"Oya."

"You know the rules of entry. You may not gain entry through me until you complete the riddle I give to you." Yaga had solved many such riddles over the years, and she had no fear of them now. She simply nodded at Oya respectfully. "There are two sisters: one gives birth to the other and she, in turn, gives birth to the first. Who are the two sisters?"

Yaga knew the answer but gave a reasonable amount of time before answering. To answer too quickly might incur Oya's wrath. Kass glanced at Yaga nervously as the seconds ticked by. She hadn't let him in on the secret. The clouds darkened overhead, swirling slowly. Kass was staring at them openly, and Yaga bumped his foot with her shoe, hopefully unobtrusively.

"The two sisters are Day and Night, Oya. Day gives birth to the moon every evening at sunset, and Night gives birth to sun every morning at dawn. Hear me, Oya. I have brought you a gift, Mother of Nine."

Oya nodded, accepting both the answer and outstretched bottle. Yaga grabbed her hand before she opened the bottle. Oya frowned at her, and her fiery clothes burned brighter as the clouds above their heads began to tumble and rotate.

"Please, Mother, let me explain my gift before you open the bottle." The fiery woman let go of the bottle's lid, and Yaga released the goddess's hand. "There is black earth, Motherland, in that bottle. But I took it from Kali's bed. I found her there as a little girl, and then she turned to dust even as I watched her."

"Is this a riddle, Yaga?"

"Not a riddle given by me, Mother. But, perhaps a riddle nonetheless."

Oya nodded, but cradled the bottle and made no attempt to open it again. Yaga didn't know what she would do with it, but this was the only goddess who dealt with the death of immortals. Yaga knew that this was the only place she could bring such an item. She had been uncomfortable even holding it on the way here, uncomfortable gathering the earth and ashes from Kali's bed. She had been afraid that she would arrive to find that even the Mother of Nine had been taken.

"Mother," Yaga paused, "I am hoping that you are not aware of the many Crones who have been taken recently."

"I am aware, but not personally. Kali is not the first to cross these boundaries. But there haven't been many. The rest are still out there somewhere. You said their ravens returned with messages intact?"

This was good news honestly, but disturbing. Who had ever found a way to restrain a goddess of death? But, they were out there at least. She was not alone.

"Yes, all the ravens returned."

"Yaga, thank you for letting me know." Oya turned the bottle over in her hand reverently. "I will take care of her. Did you leave the rest there?"

"I did, Oya. I didn't know what else to do. I don't take care of immortals."

"Was she in her home?"

"Yes, and as far as I know, she is still there. I brought what I could."

Oya nodded. "You left a person-shaped heft of the

Motherland's black earth in an immortal's house. What did you think might happen with that?" The clouds, already dark, growled ominously. "That boy you were so concerned with? How do you think someone gained control of him? How do you think he followed you, even with your suspicious Baba Yaga eyes?"

Yaga hung her head. "Oya, I will do whatever needs to be done. Tell me what to do."

"I have already been there, been and gone while you and Kass jackjawed your way here. You had the chance early on to stop this entire debacle from happening, but you couldn't make your mind up. You had to wait and see, didn't you? Since when does Yaga take mercy on a child without good cause?"

The growling clouds lurched towards the ground like a leashed hound. Yaga could see the ropy leash leading back up into the clouds, barely holding on to the vicious beast at the other end. Beneath the torrent, Yaga stood unyielding. Oya tilted her head back and screamed at the clouds, ripping them apart to release the lightning. The entire sky was a storm, and Yaga bowed her head finally under its wrath. They made their way back to the gate, backs bent beneath the onslaught. Lightning forked to the ground, as though to chase them away from Oya's displeasure.

Yaga's storm was not one to be beaten. Amplified with Kass's strength, the two storms collided, one cold and one hot. In the center line, the boundaries were angrily conflicted. Yaga's power was running high, and Oya hadn't even noticed that her aged Crone nature was retreating. Yaga's temper rose, her storm still building. She may have bowed her head, but it wasn't in her nature.

The two storms were monstrous: swirling and grumbling grotesque shapes. Oya stood on the hill behind them, fiery robes swirling around her legs, twisting around her ankles. She was all colors at once, where Yaga was grey. Yaga could take that fire, she knew it. Kass was watching the exchange, reading Yaga's mind by reading the clouds, ever more unsettled.

"Jez, you cannot."

"Oh, but I can."

"Then you should not. Oya is not your enemy. Do not get distracted. That temper you feel, that hot current of need, that is the sap of youth running through your body. All it causes is trouble; do not listen to it." Kass calmed her, with one eye on the clouds overhead. He knew that no one should trust Yaga, not even those closest to her. She was visibly shaking, fists clenched, and he knew that the battle within must be formidable. Everything Yaga did was formidable, but it was easy for him to forget that when he looked at her.

She didn't look formidable; she looked delicate and feminine. She was scrawny, though he had seen how much she was eating in these past few days. She had long hair, coarse and thickly wavy; it flowed like a dark river across her shoulder and down her back. Her hair was a hypnotic snake, but he restrained himself as he had counseled her with Oya. This wasn't the Jezi he knew, but it would be eventually, and he didn't want to pay the taxes that this transgression might incur later. He tried to shake it off, focusing on helping her shake off her own effects. She didn't need to jump into conflicts with other goddesses right now. He needed to help get her mind back on track.

With open palms, outstretched towards her, he pled the case. "Oya is not against us, Jez. She should be upset with what has happened, but I do not think she believes that you are the source of that. She is angry, and that is her domain. That is her right and her function, just as your function is the transport of souls from life to death, from nothing to life. You must allow her this. It is not focused on you."

Yaga shuddered under the valiant attempt. The clouds above rippled in response, and began to weaken. Oya's storm continued to rage, and battered the smaller storm, but found less fuel to feed itself on. The woman's robes faded to a mere shimmer, and her storm calmed to a shower. When the soft rain finally broke on them, it broke Yaga's stupor. She crossed back over the boundary, leaving Oya's territory and returning to the mortar and pestle to take Kass home.

She looked over her shoulder at the woman watching on the hill. "Oya, hear me." In response, Oya simply inclined her head, acknowledging Yaga's words. "I would know who has done this. I will strike balance. You care for the lost, but I will take care of the equilibrium that has been shattered in the meantime."

"This is not yours, Yaga. Kali was one of mine to care for."

"I do not take her from you. I claim my own. The balance, I must strike at whoever has upset. I doubt not that whoever claimed Kali, whoever stole her power, is the same one behind the other goddesses who have been taken."

To this, Oya dipped her head. "Do this then, child."

"You already knew some of this. Point me, what do you know?"

"I can only tell you to look for anyone still standing. Follow the power, it is draining somewhere." She looked pointedly at Yaga now, as well as at Kass. "Do not let anyone go unpunished simply for the connection you think you feel to them. If you become the hunter, the punisher, you must bring justice to whoever has asked for it."

"Yes, Mother."

"You are not simply Baba Yaga now. You are no longer Crone; you are the Bone Mother. Go find the one who has desecrated them." And Yaga felt the power in herself rise."Yaga has only ever been one of your names." Great black birds burst from the trees behind them. As Yaga turned again, her shadow loomed larger somehow than before.

They returned home in silence, and Yaga's eyes remained closed the entire trip; no word was spoken. They returned home, but Yaga didn't go inside with Kass. She walked directly into the woods, into the snow and trees and barren winter landscape. He let her go.

She spent three nights outside, and Kass kept the store closed. He lit the fireplaces so that when she did come back in, she would come in to a warm, living home. He didn't want her to lose herself in this new identity, however necessary it might be to her purpose. He has always known that Yaga was bigger. She was never just a kitchen witch, never simply a scary story for children, never an old witch woman who dealt in potions. And now, she was not simply a Crone. She had crossed backwards into the boundaries that she had helped so many to cross. Yaga was a Mother of many.

CHAPTER FIVE

The trees stood like skeletons, backlit by the grey snow of twilight. A dense fog hung between the land and the sky, and the waiting time stretched to fill what seemed an eternity. Inside the home, Kass could hear clocks ticking away the seconds, the minutes, the hours; outside was eternity. The birch trees were sentinels on the edge of a battlefield. He wasn't sure what battle Yaga was fighting out there, and he didn't know how to help. Instead, he kept tending fires and cooking meals she could return to. Kass was out of his element. He was meant to be ferocious, to wield storms in the same manner that Yaga did. He had frightened men from their bones in his own day, but since those days, Kass had shrunk. He was no longer Koschei the sorcerer, the whirlwind, the terrifying shape-shifter, the farseeing. He was older than Yaga, though he had never been more powerful than her, and she had never seen fit to comment on it. And so he waited, diminished, while she grew in strength, three full days and three full nights.

He wasn't sure how he had ended up with Yaga, looking back on it. He had been powerful in his own right. One thing led to another, and he had found himself tied to her over the years, passively accepting the drudging toil of time. At one point, he had been in her service, but now they were something closer to friends. It was always hard to say with Yaga though. One day friends, but on the next she would task him like a servant again. Somehow, he always complied, even though under the surface he had long been at a simmering boil.

The morning that she came back out of the forest, she walked out from the trees, diminutive in stature, but nature recognized her for what she was. The trees changed as she moved between them. This Yaga brought death with her, and the trees changed as she moved between them, turning brittle, dead now where before they slept the winter sleep. This was Yaga the Bone Mother, the Black Goddess, and her footsteps shook the earth. She brought chaos out of that forest, and Kass felt the force of it in his bones.

Kass saw that she walked barefoot now, having discarded her shoes somewhere in the snow. Despite himself, he felt his spine tingle, the hair on the back of his neck prickle. She walked directly to him, as if she had known he would be there. He knew now; she wouldn't come sit by the fire, and she wouldn't eat the food that he had prepared for her return. The Jezibaba who had walked into the forest was not this dark goddess before him. He stood and waited while she approached. He tried not to shiver, and he wished for a tenth of the power he had let go so many ages ago. She was a dwarfing presence, reminding him that it had been a long time since he had wished to have all that back.

"Close your eyes, Koschei." Her words snapped like a whip in the cold air, and he felt their sting, but decided against the many smart replies that sprang to mind. None of those felt appropriate now, he thought. He closed his eyes.

"Close them again." He didn't ask her, because he already knew. She wanted him to see, to far-see. He had not attempted this for many years; there was no need for it in this modern world where televisions would far-see for him. But he tried. His eyes were already closed, and he attempted to close them again, the act of closing off the distractions of the world around him. He shut off the flow of words in his mind: the worry, the fear, the jealousy, the pettiness, the women, the hunger for power. And then he began to see. It was like trying to see through water. Shapes were indistinct and slow. Farseeing required patience, without which the visions could be easily misinterpreted. He saw a young girl, long dark hair, but he couldn't tell who it was.

"Out with it, Koschei. What do you see?"

"A girl, young, dark hair. Dark like night. She is surrounded by ravens." He winced as he said it, because that could describe the Yaga who stood before him now. She arched a winged eyebrow at him like an irritated bird. He opened his eyes to gauge her reaction.

"Tell me more."

His eyes snapped shut. It took a moment for the haze to retreat. He struggled to shut them again, but the world around him intruded. The figure remained stubbornly hidden. "Jez, I can't. It's not clear. It's been too long since I've tried to do this."

"This isn't the type of thing one forgets. Try it again."

He kept his eyes closed, but could not force the image. He couldn't manage shutting his mind again to make the image more clear. "I need to try by myself. I think I'm just seeing you." This was not going well. She narrowed her eyes at him. "Not like that, Jezi. I'm struggling to shut everything off. I'll do it again. Alone" She didn't like his answer, but he wasn't asking permission. Without response, she swept past him, walking back towards the house. He sat there with his mouth still open for the word that was meant to come out next, when she turned around. She didn't say anything, she just looked at him. She waited long enough, with full eye contact, to make her point, and then she continued walking towards the house. He looked back at the forest one last time, wondering what happened in those three long days and nights. And then he followed her. She didn't check on him, and she didn't say anything. The two walked together, yet apart.

Kass opened the back door to the house, walking inside, but he didn't see her anywhere. Attempting to shrug off Yaga's difficult nature, he sat down at the table and closed his eyes, lifting his face as though catching the last rays of sunshine in the summer. The clock ticked away, and he sat there, and then got up and closed the window before sitting back down. After another moment he got up again to adjust the sink tap, doing away with a slow drip. And sat. And waited. And fiddled. And twitched. He caught himself drumming his fingers on the table.

She finally lost her patience and snapped at him. "Damnit, Koschei. Fine. I'm leaving."

Yaga was in the way. He couldn't see around her expanded presence. Once she was gone, truly gone, he closed his eyes, and then he closed them again. And he saw her again. She did look like Yaga, but now he could tell the difference. They had both changed, but Morgana had always had the ability to change. Jezi had never cared, but that other one, she had always lusted after youth. She was Crone, but she could shift on a whim, and she usually chose beautiful. This, however, was significantly younger than she had looked before. He had already known who he would see, now he just had to decide what to tell Jez.

He needed to talk to Jezi, but she hadn't returned yet. The only other person in the shop with him shouldn't be there. He wouldn't have known if he hadn't had his eyes closed. There was a shadow here. If he opened his eyes he would lose it, so he stood up, eyes closed, and moved slowly in its direction. He had far-seen it dart past the door, headed down the hall towards Jezi's bedroom. It was here looking for her, and he knew exactly who it belonged to. The shadow moved through the hall, along the wall at crazy angles, and then turned the corner without ever leaving the wall. He was sure he knew who was behind this, and he needed to find Yaga before this thing did.

He followed silently, blindly, unwilling to take his second eyes off it for a moment. He worried that if he stopped watching, if he metaphorically blinked, he would lose that shadow. Shadows could not see or hear, but he couldn't help feeling the fear that shadows carried with them. He tried to keep the fear at bay, as he focused on blindly navigating the furniture and piles of whatnot junk around Jez's house. It was hard to remember that he didn't have to be sneaky. All he had to do was keep his eyes closed to maintain the connection. The shadow continued to slink, and Kass continued to follow. He knew something the shadow didn't. Yaga was not here.

He watched it seeking for Yaga, probing with shadow fingers. This wasn't the first time he had come into contact with one of these; it wasn't the first time he had seen them alone. It was the first time he had seen one who wasn't looking for him. Kass's only advantage right now was that he had happened to be far-seeing when the shadow came into the house.

He was almost sad that Yaga wasn't here; the confrontation would have been priceless. Kass could only watch and hope that Jez got impatient and came back to goad him into action sooner than expected. The shadow slipped around the walls, spreading out over the bed, under the bed, and inside the closet for a moment. Having not found what it was searching for, the shadow slipped back out of the room. The search continued across every wall, and Kass dogged its every step. A full hour he trailed it through her home, and Yaga never showed. Finally, the shadow left to return to its owner. Kass knew that it would speed home under the moonlight, to reattach itself with a bit of magic, thread, and soap. Only homemade soap worked though; store-bought soap was missing a certain something.

Kass waited at the door as it went, closing it once the shadow was out of sight. And right on cue, Yaga walked in. "Alright Kass, times up. Let's talk."

Kass became more irritated. He understood that this was a time for desperate measures, but she was treating him like a tool at her service. Kass had his own standing and wanted to be appreciation for his own abilities. He had never once complained about his secondary status to her.

"Ok, but Jezi, you need to know —" She cut him off.

"I know what I need to know about, Kass. It's stuck in your head. I need you to unlock it and tell me what you saw. I gave you plenty of time. Quit playing games, and let's move this along."

He growled. "Look Jezi. I get it. I do. This is important stuff, and I know you need what I have. I have other things I need to share with you too though."

Yaga's shoulders and the subtle tilt of her head betrayed her unwillingness, but her words simply said, "Let's hear it then, Kass. But let's hear the far-seeing first, shall we?"

And he was beaten again. She was the black goddess, and he was simply a sorcerer.

"I saw her, Jez. I saw Morgana, but she is young like you. Like us," he corrected.

"Which would make sense, Kass, but I have already been to see her, and she was missing like the others."

"Isn't it possible that she wasn't missing, she just wasn't there? The person I saw was definitely her. You need to go find the Morrigan. I warned you before that you shouldn't trust her."

Yaga nodded, but displeasure wasn't the emotion he saw in her face. He had expected something a little different from what he saw in that moment. It was as though she had known this moment was coming and had long since reserved the steel reinforcement to carry her through. She didn't even flinch.

"The Morrigan it is. I will go pay a visit. By myself," she told him, in case he had any ideas of tagging along to make sure he got his own vengeance in.

"Someone, and probably her, sent a shadow tonight," he said, finally.

Yaga's head jerked up. "A shadow, here?"

Kass nodded. "It was here for about an hour, searching for you."

"A shadow here? For an entire hour?"

While there were those who could work shadow magic, there were few who could control it over long distances and hold it to a task over that distance for an entire hour. Kass looked cagey, but she put it down to tracking the shadow for such a long time. Time for Yaga to hunt again.

The Morrigan had been busy, but she had to come home sometime. Every goddess was drawn to her own hearth. She might stay away for awhile, busy with the business of her worlds, but eventually, she would return. Yaga intended to wait her out here. She let herself into the house, and settled at Morgana's kitchen table with a cup of coffee, so that she could be close to the door. The house was darkened and felt unused. Yaga had been hoping there was a misunderstanding, that Morgana had gotten mixed up in something, or was out causing trouble that would turn out to be unrelated.

Yaga wasn't sure how long she waited, but she knew the shadow was here waiting too. She couldn't see it, but she could feel it. It was uncomfortable knowing something else was moving in an empty house with her. She shifted in her chair, attempting to settle her nerves. Morgana would be back soon. She would know that her shadow had found Yaga, but she wouldn't know where. Yaga wanted to use the surprise to its best advantage.

When Morgana came home, she didn't use the front door. No sensible witch ever did. As soon as she opened the door, her shadow was at her side, a dog waiting for its master to return. It didn't want to be reattached; apparently freedom was nice, even for a shadow. It took some discipline, and some extra soap, to get it reattached, as well as time for it to stop struggling and settle down to its typical shadow ways. Yaga waited. She watched Morgana struggling with the prosaic task from where she sat.

"Silly shadows, they never want to go back home completely, do they?" Yaga chuckled darkly from her perch, "You give them a bit of independence, and then you have to rein them in to make them behave. I guess it's true about anyone."

Morgana had the presence of mind not to jump out of her skin. She turned calmly to acknowledge the woman sitting in the dark unannounced. "Yaga."

"Morrigan."

At the name, the woman's face shimmered between her three selves, a budding young girl, a voluptuous mother, and a bony Crone. It seemed to Yaga that this woman couldn't decide what she wanted to be.

"Power is a funny thing, Morgana. They say it has a corrupting force."

"Yes, yes. I've heard. Something about power corrupts —" she broke off and changed tactic. "So, what brings you here?" Morgana purred. Her eyes glinted dangerously in the low light, but Yaga sipped on her coffee disinterestedly.

"We haven't seen you in awhile. Been busy?"

"We? You have Kerridwen with you somewhere? I must have missed her." Morgana looked around with feigned innocence, wide doe eyes on her too youthful face.

"You didn't miss her."

Morgana's lips spread in something that looked like a smile. Yaga smiled back aggressively.

"Why are you here, Jezi?" Morgana asked again, teeth clenched on the name. Cheeky thing, her mannerism had definitely changed. She was less in control of herself, emotional, visibly restrained. Yaga could use this to her advantage. She didn't know what Morgana had gotten into, but by the looks of it, this time the trouble had gotten too big.

"What have you done, Morrigan?" Yaga wasn't going to use friendly names now. That time had passed. She was upset though, inside. Morgana had been her friend, the one she had felt she truly connected to, among all the others. She and Morgana had been kindred spirits, but now Morgana was on the wrong side of balance, the one thing that Yaga held sacred.

"What have you done?" Yaga repeated.

"I have found a way to stay young forever, Jezi. There are so many who perform the same function to the world; we cannot possibly need such replication of purpose. I took the lesser ones out first, and then I waited. I was so careful, so clever. I waited to see what, if any, effect my dalliances would have on the balance on the world." She looked to Yaga to see what effect her words were having.

Yaga had long ago learned to school her face to silence. Her expression would tell no tales that she didn't want told. Morrigan searched for evidence of Yaga's thinking, whether she was for or against, whether she had anything to fear. Yaga wasn't ready to let that information go just yet.

"I didn't understand it at first, I think because the power was so spread out. But, once I started, I had to find out what would happen. It became a manic need, and I had to tip the scales, just to see." She paused, and Yaga could feel it coming. "It wasn't until I passed ten or so that I started to feel it. I have always been able to alternate between young and old, as I pleased, but I was tired of it feeling like a disguise. As I killed the goddesses, I felt youth in my blood. I cannot even change form now — this is all I have."

Yaga had seen her shimmer into the different forms, so she didn't think that Morgana understood as much of what was going on as she thought she did. This arrogance was a common error in those who possessed youth and youthful beauty instead of age and wisdom. But she nodded anyway. Morgana looked encouraged and continued on.

"It was intoxicating. I loved it so much that I had to have more. I was afraid that it might be reversible. Then came the day that I found out I could not become a Crone anymore. Now, I cannot be Mother or Crone. Maiden only for me, and couldn't be more pleased." Yaga wondered at that, since she knew the threads of balance intimately. She knew what a woman sacrificed in order to gain the peace and wisdom and security of age. She had never thought the trade off that important. Morgana however, had always felt the sting.

"By the way, Jez, you look great." Yaga grunted. She was becoming concerned about Morgana's mind. Apparently this transformation wasn't only physical. She hadn't noticed it in herself yet, other than the apparent hormones that had been running rampant through her body, but it was starting to make sense.

Yaga frowned at the Morrigan. "If I could undo what I see in myself, I would. I think that everyone who is left is suffering from the same affliction. You have effectively consolidated the power into fewer bodies." Yaga thought back on her original theory: the visit to Father Time and his concentric stone circles. "Did you make any other visits, before you starting stalking all the Crones?" Yaga forced herself to keep eye contact with the Morrigan.

"Oh I'm out of Crones. I have moved on to Mothers."

"Focus, Morgana. Did you visit anyone else, before you made the decision to start all this?"

Morgana sat down, her rounded cheeks blushed with the effort it took to focus. She pursed her lips, and she looked up at the ceiling. "Before we talked? Or after?"

"Either, sweetie," Yaga's breath whispered between her teeth as she struggled not to grind them together.

"I had been thinking. I already had my plans set up then. I meant to tell you girls everything and then— I don't know. I wasn't feeling it. I was sure that either you or Kerridwen would nix my plans, try to tell me that it was morally wrong and all that. So I simply didn't bother to tell either of you."

Yaga had known that night that something else was in the air. Morgana's invite had sounded more important than the night of scrying that they had ended up sharing. It had felt like juvenile witchery at the time, which made so much more sense now. It wasn't just Morgana's face and her body; even Morgana's mind was juvenile. She was so obsessed with her physical youth that her entire identity was turning back in time.

"Did you go visit the Father for any reason?" Yaga reminded her again of the question at hand.

"Oh sure I did. I asked him what the punishment would be for killing another immortal." She didn't laugh so much as she giggled, and the sound made Yaga's skin crawl. "I didn't tell him I was considering it, and he made the consequences sound dire. But he ended with this statement. He told me that if someone took it upon themselves to end the lives of those who live forever, the scales of justice would choose something to take away from them as well. I asked him if he meant their life. He said the scales choose something precious. I took that to mean that I would have to make a sacrifice, but I wouldn't have to give up my life. I decided that it was worth it. So I asked the two of you over, and the scrying showed me what would happen after I took a few lives." She pouted a bit before she continued. "Of course, my original goal was the power I would gain. I didn't know I would get this too." She ran her hands down the curves of her body, distracted again.

The inside of Yaga's head was screaming for blood. The little chit sat here talking about scales of balance as though it were a cash register: you give, you take. There were such subtle forces at play, it was a wonder her ignorance hadn't unmade the world at this point. Yaga couldn't see the Morgana she had known before. That woman had been her friend, more her friend than any person she had ever met. Yaga wasn't built for friendship, but in the Morrigan she thought she had met someone so like herself, that their common ground granted them a relationship. And for many a year, it had worked. This creature who sat before her now, this thing, was not the Morrigan. She didn't know what had changed exactly, but she was going to feel no remorse. She would feel something more akin to pleasure, and the scales cried out for justice. Her hands fairly twitched with it. With all the blood she had split, this woman would be extremely powerful, close to the same level as Yaga herself.

CHAPTER SIX

One third of the Morrigan sat before her now: arrogant and hormonal, intolerable and self-righteous. Morgana didn't notice; she was so full of herself and the telling of her triumph. Outside, the wind howled. Yaga could not think of her as Morgana. This thing was corrupted inside and out, and while it may have once been her friend, that was no longer the case. The way Yaga saw it, the woman she knew as Morgana had died a long time ago. The All Father must have seen it coming, when he gave the cryptic warning about what she would have to sacrifice. In the intensity of her desire, Morgana had misread the warning.

"Why, Morgana? Why would you want this?" Yaga felt her skin might blister with the heat of her rage. Yaga could hardly herself in check. The wind peaked and rattled the windows in their frames.

"Are you kidding? Why would I not? Have you seen me?" The windows sounded like they might break, but still Morgana didn't notice.

"What about what you have given up?"

"What, wrinkles? Grey hair? I've gained the attention of every man that I pass."

"Is this worth more to you? You were powerful in your own right, Morgana. You were intense, and you were fascinating. Can you even work spells anymore? Maybe that's why you can't change to your other forms anymore. Did you think of that? Those other parts of you, they are all locked away now, lost."

"I haven't lost anything that I wanted more than this, Jez. I am immortal. I still hold the power that I held before." The wind clawed at the windows, desperately trying to find a way into the house. Even Yaga winced at the sound.

Do you still hold the power that you think you do, I wonder, Yaga thought.

Morgana tossed her pretty black hair and looked coyly at Yaga. "Tell me you don't love this, Jezi. Tell me you aren't reveling in the youth I have given you. I had thought you'd be the one right at my side, Jezi. I thought you hated the way you have to live—all alone in a little hut in the woods, where parents send the children they don't want so that you will gobble them up, or whatever it is that you do." She tossed her hand to the side dismissively.

Yaga grunted. Morgana wouldn't understand. This Morgana wouldn't understand anyway. Yaga wasn't a wicked witch in a hut hidden away in the woods who ate up lost children; she was a primeval force of chaos, life, death, and change. And she wasn't going to pretend to be Jezi anymore.

Yaga was coming back into her own. The wind continued to howl as Yaga's mind wrestled with her choices. She couldn't allow Morgana to continue. She couldn't truly expect to benefit without consequence from what she had done. Nothing in the universe happens without consequence; even good carries a price to achieve balance.

Yaga was the universe; she was the sky goddess stretched out like a roof, her belly made of stars, protecting and sheltering the earth. Her bones were said to be made of iron, keeping her forever cold inside. Her appetite was legendary and voracious. Yaga's appetite and her anger seemed to grow in kind: when one increased, so did the other.

A window upstairs shattered, finally catching Morgana's adolescent attention, breaking through her self-absorption to register something from the outside world. She jumped and locked eyes with Yaga, whose face was white with the effort of keeping her temper in check. She didn't much want to, which made it difficult to master her need to lash out at Morgana. As her anger grew out of control, she was beyond saving Morgana, had she wanted to. Yaga was bigger than herself; she was the Black Goddess, and as such, her purpose consumed her. Her belly growled, and the thunder growled overhead. What happens below, is echoed above. Another window shattered, and Morgana flinched.

"Yaga." Morgana's voice was almost pleading. "What I have done is good. I have taken out unnecessary replicas. Most of those goddesses did the exact same thing that we do. It can't be necessary."

"You, child, are hardly the one to judge that for anyone." Yaga's voice was gravel, iron teeth crushing rocks in her throat. Morgana's frightened eyes darted around the room. Yaga was disgusted with her. The Morrigan she had known would never have shown fear. Everything useful had been stripped from her. The storm was descending, and the sounds of shattering glass, underscored with wild clashes of thunder, filled her ears. The chaotic symphony spurred her on to destruction. The pulse of the storm was her own, and the wind howled with the sound of her own voice.

The last window shattered; every inch of floor glittered with shards of glass. Yaga stepped over them carelessly, crushing them beneath her feet with disregard. She had backed the young girl who used to be called Morgana into a corner. Once this stupid girl had been part of a powerful trinity, one of the most powerful deities in the universe. She had been a battle goddess, flanked by an army of ravens. Her wrath was the death of nations. The Nightmare Queen was both one and threefold: war, chaos, and sovereignty. She was not death, she was the keeper of Death. Some had even called her the Irish Kali, Fata Morgana. All reduced to this.

The silver string of Yaga's patience shattered, and the hunger demanded satiety. She opened her jaws; she was a black maw, and she swallowed the thing that used to be Morgana. She took her in and ate her whole as the storm reduced the house to rubble around them. Yaga stood on the pile of broken pieces of wood, brick, and stone. It wasn't until that moment that the rain began to fall from the storm raging above. Yaga was exhausted, but finally, she wasn't hungry. Her belly was huge with the meal she had eaten. She left the house in its destroyed state, took her mortar and pestle, and headed for home. She made sure to use the broom to sweep away any evidence of herself there, though she knew that the people whose opinions mattered already knew what she had done. She didn't care. Balance had demanded it. She had no idea what to do next, but first Yaga was going to go home and sleep.

She slipped in the back door of the Rookery, a door that led into her own kitchen. It was warmly lit, and there was food on the table and a fire in the hearth. She wrinkled her nose at the smell of food, instead falling heavily into a chair by the fire. She didn't think to look around the house to see who had left everything for her. She knew. It had to have been Kass. She slept deeply, and when she woke it was dark. Grimacing, she reminded herself that everyone slept after a large meal. She groaned and closed her eyes. When she woke again, Kass was in the chair opposite. She wasn't in the kitchen anymore, but in a large chair in the sitting room, beside a new fire. She looked him over; he was impossibly young now, much like herself probably.

"What happened, Yaga?" It wasn't often that Kass referred to her as Yaga. He preferred to call her by a name rather than what he saw as a title. She sighed and closed her eyes again. When she opened them, what felt like seconds later, the light had changed again. She was still in the chair, in her sitting room, sitting by the fire. She had always loved this chair; it was overstuffed, big enough to seat two people if they really liked each other and had small personal bubbles. That wasn't Yaga though. She would settle herself into the center of it and bolster herself with pillows, or drape over onto one side of it. Now that her bones were younger, she liked to curl up into one corner and pull her legs up under her. She felt like a little cat, curled up on the chair in front of the fire. She stretched and yawned and groaned. She saw Bayun echo her stretch and yawn from the char opposite. And then she saw Kass.

He was still waiting. He sat in a chair on the opposite wall, leaving her some space while she woke up. But his eyes were full of questions. She could see the concern in his eyes as well, but he was doing a good job of covering that up for the moment.

"What happened, Yaga?"

"How long have I been asleep, Kass? Goddess, I needed that." She stretched some more, working out the kinks of what felt like days of sleep instead of hours. Which made her wonder, "How long did I sleep?"

He seemed solemn, more than usual. She must have actually scared him. "Three days."

That woke her up finally, and she sat bolt upright in the overly plush chair. No wonder she was achy. That many hours sleeping in a chair would have close on to killed her in more recent days.

"What happened, Jez?" Three times he had asked her, and everyone knew that if someone asked a question three times, they had to get what they asked for. The old days swirled in her head, and she laughed dizzily, thankful that he hadn't asked for something difficult.

He simply waited, though her mood concerned him. She didn't seem herself.

"Morgana. Morgana happened." She thought back over the memories of that night, but her mind felt muddled. She was accustomed to being able to think sharply, calling to mind any piece of information. She felt confused. And hungry.

He already had a plate of food ready and handed it to her now. It was stacked high with fluffy pancakes, drizzled with maple syrup: dark, sweet, and sticky. There were biscuits cut with butter and honey, slabs of ham, and crisp bacon crumbled into scrambled eggs. The eggs were soft and milky, the way she liked them. She hated the way that Kass cooked eggs for her, not that he ever ate any for himself, overcooked and hard yellow. He had cooked these exactly the way that she preferred them, probably tired of all the times she had thrown his offerings away. There was more food than she could possibly eat, but she soon found that she had eaten everything, including the handful of grapes and slices of melon. She drank two cups of black coffee, the strong and bitter taste balancing out the heavily fragrant tastes of breakfast.

She could feel the cold in the room receding as she ate, as though the food warmed her more than the fires. Once she was warm again, it was okay to tell him what had happened.

"She was the one who did it all, Kass. She went to see the All Father, to ask him what would happen. She was foolish enough to think that he wouldn't know she was asking for herself. He gave her a warning about sacrifices, but assured her the sacrifice wouldn't be her own life." She frowned then, because obviously Morgana had sacrificed her life at the end. She hadn't ever heard of a time that the Father of Time had been anything but brutally honest. He reveled in honesty, wielding it as a weapon at times.

"She was so young, and I could feel it in her mind. She wasn't sharp enough to match me. She talked and talked, but she was so unaware. It was hard to watch."

Kass watched her, and his hard eyes glittered.

"Have you looked at yourself, Jez?"

She frowned at him, uncomprehending. "I'm assuming that having killed likely the last veil goddess, I am quite young now. I saw Kali before she died. I saw the Morrigan before she died. They looked like children. Am I that young?"

He shook his head slightly. His face looked like he was chewing on something he wanted to say but couldn't manage to spit out.

"Perhaps you should go look, Jez."

She rolled her eyes, and then caught herself. She had seen Morgana's mistake, discounting everyone else around her. She probably should go look.

In the mirror, she only recognized her eyes. "It couldn't be helped," she assured him, but she continued to search her reflection. Her skin was smooth as milk, with flushed cheeks and sparkling eyes. Her eyelids didn't droop; nothing sagged. She smoothed her fingers over her face, wondering at the freshness of life that she could feel. She ran her fingers through her hair, lifting it back and away from her face; it felt heavy and thick. She could feel its coarseness, betraying what would happen to it later, but it didn't change the miracle of its beauty now.

She ran her fingers down her throat, still watching her reflection. She could tell that it was herself, the mirror matched her every move, but it was like watching a stranger. She had never once, never in her long immortal life, been young. She had never known the delicateness, the ignorance, the intoxication of it. She could almost see how Morgana had lost herself. With a moment of hesitation after the thought occurred to her, she hooked a finger into the neck of her shirt. She looked into the shirt thoughtfully, before letting it fall again from her fingers.

But that's when she saw it. Kass hadn't been awed by her youth. He also had experienced that effect. He had been asking her to see the rest. Her belly was still huge, grotesquely deformed apart from the slimness of the rest of her body. Poor Kass, he didn't know how the story ended, so there is no telling what he thought.

She turned to look at him.

"Yes, that," he confirmed.

"I'm not sure how to explain, but I promise it will go away."

His eyebrow jumped. "You look pregnant, Jez. And you look fifteen. It's hard for me to look at. It's hard for me not to look at," he emphasized.

"I can't explain it exactly. It's not what you think though.

Morgana and I, we—" she stopped, not sure how to confess the horrific nature of what she had done. She spread her hands out before her, as though in supplication for his understanding. "It's not the first time I've done this."

He shifted his shoulders a bit. "Had a child? It most certainly is."

She looked away. She loooaked at her belly, at the illogical evidence of the night before. "It's not a child."

"Oh gods, Jezi! You ate her?" Kass covered his face with his hands.

"It happened so quickly, and it felt like it wasn't the one in control in the moment." They sat in silence. She wasn't sure what to say, and he didn't want to look at her. "What's done is done, and she brought this on herself. I'll tell you the whole story later."

She shifted mental gears with difficulty. "I have to ensure that the Balance is restored. I'm not sure what happens to all those who have been taken." Morgana had killed a great many goddesses in her quest for youth, and she wasn't the first to try out the theory. Old stories were thick with witches and sorceresses who killed young girls to steal their youth. Morgana had taken the old stories another step, as she always did, playing the idea out to its absolute limits. "I think I'll go speak with Grandmother."

Only one of the aged goddesses had transcended Crone. She was older than anyone Yaga knew, excepting perhaps Father Time. "She will know what I need to do to remedy what has happened. She sees how everything is connected; she spins the connections between them herself. If something is still broken because of

Morgana's hand, Grandmother will know."

Kass nodded miserably but maintained his silence.

"Anyway, I think I have eaten and slept plenty, so I will leave straight away. Grandmother lives quite far away." Yaga gathered some food for the trip in a basket. With as hungry as she had been lately, she doubted that she would make the trip without nourishment. She packed the basket with breads and hard cheeses, a bottle of water, a thermos of coffee. On second thought, she also slipped in a bag with sliced meats to pair up with the cheese and bread. She hesitated with her hand hovered over the handle to the pantry door, but stopped herself. No need to overindulge.

CHAPTER SEVEN

Since Grandmother lived in the caves, preferring to be away from the modern shininess of this world, Yaga packed a heavy woolen hooded cape. The caves would be cold, and the cold had never been her friend. She had reached for her favorite coat, but doubted that it would fit around her protruding belly. She frowned down at it; she had hoped that would be receding by this time. The cape fit nicely though, and she imagined that it helped hide the belly a bit. If Grandmother had lived only inside town somewhere, Yaga could have taken the Shadow instead. Even if she had decided on more modern transportation, she would still have had to trek far into the mountains where Grandmother lived. Yaga pouted, petulant, at the thought. There was nothing for it though, so into the mortar she went.

Flying brought Yaga back to herself when she became too absorbed in the details of life in that year, that generation, that century. Flying in a mortar and pestle was so quintessentially Yaga that it couldn't help but turn her mind inwards. As she rose farther into the sky, the cold air brought Yaga's head out of the metaphorical clouds. She could feel the distractions like fog in her head, clouding her judgment. Thoughts scurried like wild animals, difficult to corral or manage. It felt impossible to do anything but surrender to the chaos. She refused; regardless of her current youth, inside she was still Baba Yaga. She was bigger than this. Nonetheless, she could not wait to be old again.

The land rushed away from her, valleys and rivers and coasts and prairies. Mountains staggered across the dark horizon. The stars looked like holes pricked into the black fabric of the night, where light from beyond shone through. Looking down, she could almost see the webs connecting everything, all streaming together here at the center point where Grandmother lived and spun. Yaga guided the vessel down from the starry heights into the depths of the mountains.

Grandmother did not enjoy company or distractions. Likely, Yaga's visit would not please her, but hopefully she would understand the necessity. Yaga left her broom in the mortar, just outside the opening to Grandmother's cave. She wasn't sure what to expect, as she had never visited the woman before. She was hoping that while the outside was made of rock carved by millennia, the inside might have running water, carpets, and heaters.

The cave was damp and dark and rank. Grandmother must not be the only one living here. Yaga continued to walk, pleased she had thought to bring a flashlight. She waited as long as she could to turn it on, until there was no light to guide her feet. With the flashlight on, she could only see exactly where it pointed; the bright light was almost worse than the darkness. Another few steps proved her wrong. Having turned a few corners and descended to a great depth, there was absolutely no natural light. She grew concerned that there might be a drop or a trap of some kind. She slowed her pace and examined her path carefully before continuing on each time.

The cold seeped into her bones as she moved farther in and further down. Had there been enough light, she could have seen her breath in the cold air. She pulled her cape closer and brought the hood up over her ears. Her eyes were tiring from the effort of peering into the dark and the one bright circle. Ahead she thought she saw the faintest glow. It was impossibly placed, ahead and high to the right. She shook her head and closed her eyes for a moment to rest them.

Yaga continued down the path, training the white circle onto her path as she went. Her pace slowed to a crawl as the path began to climb. The light she had seen was growing more distinct, less like an apparition. This must be Grandmother's House finally. She kept walking until she could switch off the flashlight, at which point light from the opening seemed blinding to her eyes.

Grandmother would have known she was coming, but she wasn't here. Yaga decided to stand and wait, rather than sit anywhere. Other than being large, the furniture oversized, the room was oddly normal. There were rugs after all and electric light, which was both odd and comforting. There were strange things hidden among the normalcy. On a shelf of knick-knacks there might also be a beetle carapace. Plates hung on a wall in true grandmotherly fashion, but they were decorated with sugar skulls. Woven tapestries warmed the effect of bare stone, but had Aztec sacrifices woven into the designs. The collective effect was truly unsettling.

Yaga contented herself to look around the room. She knew better than to sit without permission; it was the same type of mistake she would have caught visitors for in her own domain. Everything was a potential trap that would result in the visitor leaving without what they came for. She didn't intend that to be the outcome here.

She could hear Grandmother moving in the other room. "Grandmother, I am Baba Yaga come to visit you," she announced, so that it wouldn't seem that she was sneaking around. It was difficult to be on unequal footing, something Yaga wasn't used to. It was even more difficult to remember that she was an equal, not a stripling of a girl come to curry favors. Youth did not favor her, Yaga decided.

"Thank you for coming to visit me, sweetling." Grandmother's voice was raspy and decidedly odd. "I don't have many visitors, as you can imagine. Recently though? I can't seem to shoo enough away."'" She chuckled, and the sound was dry, sticks rubbed against stone. Yaga could hear her moving closer. Her skin was trying to crawl away, and she had to school herself to stillness.

She shook herself mentally. *You are Baba Yaga. Do not disgrace yourself in the presence of an old one. You may look like a girl, but you are not. Quit acting like one, and get yourself together.*

By the time Grandmother entered the room, Yaga had managed to pull herself together. She held her chin up at a respectful balance between self-assured and insolent, being careful not to cross the boundary on either side. In either direction lay offense and injury.

"May I offer you anything to eat, child?"

Yaga shook her head respectfully. Every interaction was a step in the dance, and no one understood that better than she. That said, she was struggling not to stare. She had never met the Grandmother before, though she had heard stories. It was no wonder that few came to visit. The woman would stand out more than Kali would have. She too was completely black, but shiny. Her head and torso were that of a woman, though not as elderly as Yaga had expected. It was the rest of her that brought Yaga's mind to a skittering halt. Grandmother was a spider.

She had eight legs, a shiny black thorax, and a large abdomen that swung around behind her as she walked through the house. The size of the room made more sense now, Yaga reflected. Beneath her torso, beneath properly folded hands, Yaga could see poison fangs. The woman wore a shawl made of a translucent grey fabric, light as air, likely spun from her own silk. As she walked, her eight legs made a tapping sound. The sound made Yaga's nerves scream. She would never have imagined that a spider would make a sound walking.

"Have you seen your fill, Baba Yaga?"

"I mean no disrespect, Grandmother. You are quite intimidating, but there is a dangerous beauty as well. I only meant to observe."

Grandmother Spider nodded at her. The answer was an honest one, and that pleased her. "What would you know of me then, Yaga?"

"You know of what has happened with the Crones?"

"Of course child. I was at the loom when their threads snapped loose." She bristled at the impertinence of someone working with the threads who hadn't woven them. It hadn't been a well-thought out question, or rather, it hadn't been a well-phrased question. Yaga had not meant it as a literal question; she was going to have to be more careful.

"My apologies, Grandmother. I meant no offense."

The woman nodded, but one of her legs tapped impatiently. "I know what happened, perhaps better than you do. I also know your part in it." The sharp staccato beat underlay everything she said.

Yaga bowed her head in response to this. There was no denying that she had made a mistake with Morgana as regarded Grandmother Spider. It wasn't an immortal's place, any immortal, to take the life of another divinity, regardless of rank and stature. While Yaga had a responsibility to her role in the Balance, she had likely overstepped her bounds in addressing the Morrigan.

"I'm worried that I might have overstepped my authority with Morgana, Grandmother. When I went to see her, I was overcome."

Grandmother Spider accepted this thoughtfully. "You did. And you came here to make it right." This also pleased her. Yaga accepted this, though it hadn't been her intention in coming.

"Grandmother, I would ask you a question to help me address the Balance. All the Crones who preside over Death have disappeared, excepting myself. I have been told that they may not be dead, but in hiding or captured. How many are left?"

"There is only you Yaga. Whoever you spoke to was mistaken."

"Oya Yansa gave me this information."

"Then she had a reason, or perhaps at the time they were still alive. I can tell you with certainty now that they are no longer in the web."

"What is to be done Grandmother? Is there a way for me to bring them back?"

"If there is, it would not be your job."

"Am I to be alone then? Santa Muerte is gone. Kali is gone. A hundred are gone. There is Oya and myself. Oya guards the underworld, stands sentry. I am the shepherdess; I am the midwife. I cannot leave all those souls to wait for me, all those lives to be extinguished without guidance."

"Then what would you do, Yaga?"

"I would have balance restored. And it all comes back to the Crones, no matter which angle I come at it from. The whole world wants to ignore the Crones. They want youth to last forever, running between Maiden and Mother and back again."

Grandmother Spider watched her while she spoke. "And I ask you again, Yaga. What would you do?"

"I don't know!" Yaga regretted her outburst as soon as it escaped, but it wasn't that she didn't mean it. She felt lost, understanding that something needed to happen—understanding the why, but not the what, and definitely not the how. Grandmother's claw tipped leg started tapping again, and Yaga forcibly restrained her anger. "My apologies. My frustration is not with you, Grandmother. I have no idea where to go from here, and this is not something I am accustomed to."

"You are not what I had expected, Yaga. I will confess this to you."

"My mind does not feel like my own. I am meant to be Crone, and this body is Maiden."

"That body is not a Maiden, Yaga. Do not fool yourself. You may had been, but you are becoming a Mother. You had to know this, you are easily nine months with child."

The Ninth Kingdom. The Mother of Nine. The Ninth month. Yaga had let it all pass her by. Mother. This was an outcome she had never thought to expect, which seemed natural in retrospect. Grandmother Spider watched her wrestle with the revelation, with an expression that crossed between amused and fascinated. At least the leg wasn't tapping anymore.

"I understand now why your mind is not your own. You thought it was simply youth, that you lost your wisdom when you lost your Crone status. But you could not be more wrong. You have the status still, you retain your power as Yaga. You have also gained the power inherent to Maiden and Mother, something only the Morrigan should have experienced. By killing her, you took this aspect onto yourself."

Yaga boggled at this. It seemed obvious when this woman laid it out for her. She felt stupid, again not something that she was used to feeling. Yaga's mind was a finely honed weapon that she enjoyed sharpening. This was all too unexpected and presented more possibilities than she could deal with at the moment. "I just want to be Baba Yaga." She felt like crying, which made her angrier.

"I do not think you have ever been just Baba Yaga, child."

At that moment, she felt her belly move, and the whole world shifted. She had always known, underneath it all, that she was in essence a reduction of all her previous selves.

"Grandmother, what can you tell me about what happened when the threads were cut?"

"What do you wish to know, child? Be specific."

Yaga thought about it, trying to put aside all other thoughts in her head to focus. "Was it only the Morrigan? Was she the one responsible?"

"No. She didn't act alone. There was another involved. Do you wish to know?"

"I do. I must restore the balance." She paused. "It is an immortal of course."

"You will not misstep by correcting this. You didn't misstep before."

Yaga took a deep breath. That information was good to have. Did she want to know who the other was? Didn't she need to know? Even when unpleasant, this was Yaga's role. Someone had stepped outside the realm of balance and must be corrected. The weights must swing back to center.

The child she carried was a mystery that would be addressed when the time came. Who but a midwife knew better that a child would come in its own time? She laid a hand over her belly with wonder. She had helped to birth so many babies, she thought she didn't feel the quickening of wonder within herself anymore. Babies were not magical miracles; they were messy and noisy and neurosis inducing. But that had been when they were not her own. She understood the moon-eyed mothers better now than for all the centuries she had brought babies into the world.

Grandmother Spider watched her indulgently—a grandmother after all, all appearances to the contrary. She prodded Yaga gently, "Do you want to know? Think carefully before you answer. Once you know, you have to act. Your ignorance is your protection right now."

Yaga couldn't knowingly accept this. Obviously, something was out there which needed to be known, which needed to be addressed. It was something Grandmother felt that she might not want to know, might not want to face, which made her need to know all the more. She took a deep breath.

"Yes, I should know. Remove the veil of ignorance from my eyes." She felt her body shudder; she felt the first beginnings of a great ache deep within, a sense that her body wanted to open, to empty itself. She had only just found out that what she carried was a child, regardless of how it had happened. She wasn't ready to give birth yet. She willed it to stop. She had shushed every mother who said anything of the sort to her. She ignored the pains, as she knew this would take time.

Grandmother Spider gestured through a great yawning doorway with one of her legs. Such a delicate gesture, Yaga noted, wildly distracted by tiny details. She ducked her head respectfully as she passed Grandmother, who followed her through the black doorway. In the next room was a giant loom, the old fashioned wooden kind. *Even Grandmother sitting at that loom would be dwarfed*, Yaga thought. The fabric ran far away into the darkness, settling into soft folds and piles in the distance. Grandmother had been working on this for a very long time. At the foot of the loom, she could see the individual threads, silvery grey and so soft that it seemed they would snap under a breath.

"Child, touch one thread with your finger."

Yaga looked at her nervously. She knew what each thread represented and wished no harm to the person whose life was entangled with it. She shook her head slightly, wide-eyed.

Grandmother pressed her lips together. "Would I allow you to hurt anyone? Touch a thread."

Yaga put out a hand, ever so softly, and touched one of the threads that was next to be woven into the tapestry. It might look soft, but the thread was strong and felt like wire beneath her fingers. A bit of silver sparkled in places from the folds of fabric that lay across the floor. These threads shone like fine silver in the soft grey tangle of fabric.

"What are those threads?"

"Ah those. I love the effect of weaving those in. Every so often, there is a soul who shines so brightly that the whole piece is changed for having added it. Those threads do not come often."

Yaga watched Grandmother sit down to the loom. All eight of her legs settled into position, as well as her two hands. When she started weaving, the threads flashed and spun. The effect was mesmerizing. She wove quickly, but when Yaga checked the fabric, it didn't appear to have changed at all.

"The fabric moves slowly from the loom. What I weave may take ages to show its effect on the fabric you see." She continued to flicker her hands across the weft, tucking in and guiding threads individually. "I do not always get to choose the pattern, you know. Sometimes I have an idea, but the threads do not cooperate. They are stubborn, and sometimes the design is decided without me. The flaws are part of the piece as much as the design itself."

Yaga watched the threads and legs and arms flicker for a moment or two—so much movement for such little visible result. It looked like so much work for such imperceptible progress. Grandmother smiled as she worked, touching errant threads now and then to guide them into the pattern. Not every thread was cooperative. She would touch one with a finger, guiding it back into place, and sometimes she would pull or poke at it. Sometimes Yaga saw her draw a new thread together and lay it into place. It was hypnotic, and Yaga felt her mind drifting towards a sleep resembling hibernation. Time moved differently here, slower.

Grandmother's Spider's perspective was long, and Yaga was surprised and pleased that they had this in common.

The loom was a modified style of floor loom, larger than any Yaga had seen before. There were multiple treadles across the bottom of the wooden framed machine, enough so that each of Grandmother's eight feet had several to attend to. She worked them in concert, to attain some complication of design that Yaga didn't understand. She worked a shuttle through the many threads so quickly that Yaga's eye couldn't keep up. She would catch it on one side and work it through the layers in some pattern that only she recognized or remembered. At one time, the fabric at the other end had rolled onto a long piece of wood whose age Yaga could scarcely calculate. As the fabric had gotten too large that step had been ignored, and the fabric instead draped across the floor like endless sand dunes.

Grandmother Spider sat at a special seat in front of the loom, orchestrating the whole thing. It was a low seat, lower than Yaga would have guessed had she designed it, but she imagined that everything had a purpose. Looking at the wooden frame of the leviathan, Yaga could not begin to understand the system of beams and cross beams and pedals and handles. Yaga watched Grandmother Spider hum along, as completed fabric moved behind the loom into the darkness beyond.

"Would you like to try, Yaga? It is not so different from what you have done."

Yaga eyed the device doubtfully. Knowing that each piece represented a life made her less likely to try for the sake of trying.

"No, Grandmother. I wouldn't presume to be able, for any amount of time."

Grandmother Spider nodded, pleased yet again. She took up one of the bright silver threads, twisting it gently between her fingers. She looked at Yaga. "This one. This is the one who was tangled up with the Morrigan." She pointed to the thread, following its path with her fingers. "Sometimes they weave a pattern of their own. These two tangled up unexpectedly." Just past the shuttle, the two silver threads intertwined, except that one had been cut short. Grandmother had obviously been weaving around the ends to finish off the design that had been severed.

Yaga weighed the information. Knowing would change everything. Grandmother Spider waited. Yaga watched her fingers smooth the thread whose end was still loose. And then it was done, and the threads wove themselves in and around it, securing the design flawlessly. Now, it looked as though it had been meant to be this way from the beginning. She watched Grandmother Spider's fingers flit over the threads, working the silver thread she had pointed out to Yaga. Yaga tried to watch it among the multitudes of others. She kept losing it, thinking she could never possibly see one thread among all the others, and then there it would be again.

"Where is my own thread, Grandmother, if I may ask?" Yaga leaned over to peer into the fabric, thinking that one thread should call to her more than the others if it was the thread that represented her own life.

And Grandmother chuckled. "Yaga, I already showed you your own."

The inside of Yaga's head went silent, and her ears went screechy. She had the peculiar sense of being too big and too small in the same instant. The room was a cave, and it was simply a room. She watched that thread, which she now couldn't help but be drawn to. She watched how it interacted with the threads around it, how things made room, and how it worked its way into every design before disappearing again.

"So the immortals are the silver threads?"

"No child, not at all. Not all immortals are silver, not even most of them. Strangely enough, most of those silver threads are human. I have seen threads change as they progress through a design." She worked the shuttle through the rows of upstrung threads, with a rhythmic swoosh.

"There is one other whose thread you should see. It used to be silver and then it faded. Now it is as soft and grey as the rest."

Yaga looked to where the woman's fingers pointed, trying to see through the shuffle of the weft and warp. Somehow she knew who it was before Grandmother Spider told her. This was Kass. His thread was evenly spaced between herself and Morgana, something she hadn't recognized until now. At the time when Morgana's thread had been finished and woven in, Kass's thread had flashed silver again for a few iterations, fading again as it turned to weave together with her own.

This was something that would require deep thought. And sleep. And food. Suddenly Yaga was voracious, her appetite waking with a vengeance after the time she had successfully neglected it.

"One more question, Grandmother, and then I must be away. The other goddesses, have their threads been cut, or…" she trailed off. She wasn't sure what the other possibilities were that Oya had hinted at.

"Their threads are not cut Yaga, but they are not the same as they were either. The design has changed entirely."

Yaga nodded, but she did not understand. Her belly cramped again, and she winced inwardly. No need for Grandmother to know right now, but the spider woman glanced up at her and grinned wickedly as her hands worked the shuttle, the weft, and the warp. Nothing could be hidden from the woman who watched everything happen beneath her fingers. But, Yaga now knew, while she might spin the threads and weave the pattern, The Weaver didn't always have a choice in the design. The threads could change the course of events themselves, and at times, the Weaver was only one who watched.

"Go find Koschei, child. It seems you two have matters to discuss."

The fingers, the shuttle, the pedals, the eight spider feet, all moved much more quickly now, and it was obvious the Weaver had moved on. She had only slowed her actions for the benefit of an audience. She moved so quickly now that the workings of the loom were a blur beneath her.

Yaga walked back through the dark doorway into the part of the cave that looked like a house. She paused for a moment, reveling in the warmth that she felt here, before she gathered herself to walk back to the entrance. She found the flashlight again, snagged a couple cookies from the plate on the table, and gathered her bright red cloak around her shoulders again, pulling the hood up to cover her ears.

Yaga wasn't one to be defined by relationships. She existed outside of that realm, content to be one unto herself. She had never felt lonely, never sought company to relieve the solitude. She was tired of endlessly readying herself for combat. Yaga was ready to prepare herself for peace. Life had become one with the idea of hardship. She could see herself living a peaceful life. Not yet, she had things she needed to finish first, a few threads that needed to be tucked back into the pattern. Then she could rest. She hadn't known she needed it so badly. She needed sleep almost as much as she needed food.

CHAPTER EIGHT

Leaving the cave seemed much quicker. Soon Yaga was at the entrance to the cave, digging into the basket of food greedily as she flew away into the night, looking back up to the pinholes that looked like stars from the ground. She was almost asleep by the time she got home, and the basket was empty. She walked inside, feeling ragged and despondent somehow, but the lights were on and the table overflowing with food. Kass.

She didn't see him anywhere, but she ate the food. Her belly ached with hunger, then with indulgence, and then with the deep pains she was working hard to ignore. They were so far apart they were almost random, and she didn't bother to pay attention yet. She looked over the table laden with food and the fireplaces merrily burning along. She wondered if Kass had always taken care of her, or if this was only a recent development. She felt shamed that she didn't know the answer. She wondered how often Kass had felt overshadowed. Was it any wonder that he had fallen in with Morgana? And then there he was, standing in the door watching her finish eating. He didn't say anything; she watched him.

"You have been taking good care of me, Kass. I know I don't always appreciate you the way I should."

He rolled his eyes. "Don't."

"It's true though." She felt she owed him this much at least.

"Don't say it now, like you mean it all of a sudden. It doesn't change anything."

She bit her tongue and did her best not to say anything at all. She contented herself with taking another bite and chewing thoughtfully.

He didn't come to sit beside her, remaining in the doorway instead. "So, you've been to see Grandmother Spider." It wasn't a question.

She wasn't going to play soft anymore. It would have no effect here. "Quit knocking around, Kass. You already know I have. There is nothing that woman doesn't know." They both shuddered, and Yaga knew by this that Kass had been to see the woman as well. "Did you do it, Kass, or did you talk Morgana into doing it all for you?"

"My hand did nothing, Yaga."

"Which you and I both know doesn't exactly make you innocent. How did you charm her into it? I know that has to have been how you got her involved, so — What did you promise her?"

Kass looked offended. "I did my research. I knew concentrating the power would also turn the remaining divinities younger. I promised her the one thing she wanted more than anything else."

Yaga nodded and sighed. It had worried her, that a goddess able to cross between each of the three stages of life would get attached and spend her time in one. Yaga was sure that she herself would spend her time in Crone if given the choice anyway. This Mother thing wasn't working out so far, mostly fits of being tired, interspaced with being hungry, grumpy, and uncomfortable.

"And you, Jez? Let's talk about that." He pointed to her belly, which was wasn't getting smaller at all. If anything, she was bigger now than the last time he saw her.

"Yes, we'll get to that." She laid her hand on top of the damning evidence. "Later. First, let's finish talking about you." He eyed her belly pointedly. His eyes said that he felt doubtful, as though afraid the topic couldn't wait that long.

"I actually understand why Morgana did it, Kass. What I don't understand is you. What did this do for you? Why did you need her?"

He did sit down finally, reluctantly. It looked like he would have been happier to stay poised by the door for a quick getaway. "I used to be — more." He sat and nodded to himself, thinking through the enormity of what he was trying to untangle and express. "I used to be Koschei Bessmertny, the Deathless. Not immortal exactly, but I could take my death and hide it. You remember, I know you do, or you wouldn't still make those awful jokes about eggs."

Yaga winced inwardly.

"I was a powerful sorcerer, but somehow I ended up being your herdsman, and then something closer to your handyman. Was a time once, I could turn myself into the wind; I was a force of nature, destructive and powerful and terrifying. Now I fix plumbing, and I lock the doors for you when you're done playing shopkeeper." He sighed and looked around pointedly. "I could control the weather; I could fly through the air, call lightning and thunder." He paused again and watched the wood grain of the table tangle into unknowable patterns. "I was amazing and scary. Oh and I could fight, good gods could I fight. I didn't fight clean though; that was never my style. I would throw everything I had at whoever it was, and sometimes that was even you. I was vicious, downright venomous. Do you remember how long my hair was? My nails? That was part of it. I never cut anything, helped preserve my life force. Take nothing away."

Yaga watched him sadly, looking back over the time they had spent together, when all she had been concerned with was herself.

"And fighting? I always did my best work naked; I've always thought the Celts got it from me. There's power in embracing your true self, in loosing yourself from fear. The ravens used to follow me everywhere, just to pick from the scraps I left behind. They wouldn't follow armies, Jez, they would follow me. I want to be what I used to be. I'm a tired little shopkeeper for a shop that doesn't ever sell anything. So I went to Morgana, because I knew she'd be the one most likely to get into some trouble with me. What I had in mind, I knew you couldn't go along with, so I never thought of mentioning it to you."

She shook her head slightly, already frowning. She tried to clear her own reactions and listen to Koschei's story. She had to understand if she was going to know what to do with him. She could understand that he felt overshadowed, reduced, but to go from that feeling to willing to kill, to upset the balance that he knew was tenuously held, that logic she couldn't follow.

"We hatched a plan, Morgana and I. She is a violent soul," he checked himself and looked at Yaga with disapproval, " — was. But she was also a brilliant tactician. Who could think of a plan like this? Since she knew she would also benefit from it, she poured all her powers of brilliance and conniving to create a plan that could not fail. That day when you all went to tea unexpectedly, I thought she was going to let it all out, that she felt the urge to confess. What ridiculous story did she give you that night instead?"

Yaga looked at him awhile before answering, with a little cough. "It had been so long since any of us had been involved in the craft. Morgana said that she wanted to get involved again, and we fell for it. We had a night of teenage girlhood witching. I saw strange visions that night, and I had the impression that they did as well, but no one offered to share what they had seen."

He nodded at her. "I'm not surprised, because I'm sure I know what, or at least some of what, she saw. What did you see?"

"I never did know what to do with mine. I saw an old face, the kind of old that isn't even about age anymore. I had the sense that he was a hero, that he might try to kill me. Honestly, I didn't feel it as a threat, I just knew that he would show up, and that was how things would work." She thought back on that scrying, which she had forgotten about in the time since. "I have not seen him, or anything like him. First scrying I have ever seen that didn't come to pass."

"Never works that way; what is seen always comes to pass. You'll see him still."

She thought about that, and about everything that had happened between then and now. When her business was complete here, she might go hunt that man down if he wasn't on the doorstep waiting for her first. Her face went harder. There was too much to think about right now.

"What's with the belly? Pregnant? I thought this was about Morgana?"

"It is, I don't know how to explain. I promised it would go away, and it will. It might take more time than I thought." Not much more, the ache that came and went promised her. Time to make a decision. "I'm still hungry, Kass. I'm going to make myself some eggs."

He rolled his eyes but chose not to comment on that part. "How can you possibly still be hungry? I know how much you ate, I cooked it myself."

"Eating for two and all that I'm sure," she replied. She took her egg basket from the counter, and chose one. She cracked the egg, the biggest one that she been saving, into a bowl and whisked it. Kass twitched.

She poured the mixture into the skillet, on medium, and added in a bit of milk. She stirred and whisked and then left them alone, as the best eggs should be. Kass wiped the sweat from his brow.

"Nervous, Kass?"

"I will not lie, Yaga. You always make me nervous."

She cackled at that. She did like to make people nervous. The old cackle from a fifteen year old body made Kass even more nervous. She tried not to stir the eggs too much, letting them rest and cook. Kass waited at the table. "Eggs don't take long to cook. I won't be but a second." He closed his eyes.

She scooped the eggs out onto a plate and salted them slightly for flavor. She carried the plate back to the table. She settled herself back into the chair and situated her plate and her fork in front of her.

"It's not funny anymore. Overdone." He looked at her, blank faced, as she forked a bite of egg into her mouth. She chewed thoughtfully, watching Koschei's face.

"I know." She took another fork of eggs, pushing them around to pile it onto her fork for a bigger bite.

"Then why do you still do it? That's all been ages ago."

She put the fork into her mouth, testing the egg first and chewing it thoroughly before swallowing it. She pushed more egg onto her fork.

Koschei rolled his eyes again and slumped into the chair to endure whatever torture Yaga had planned for him. She took another bite of egg, and he felt a hot shock run through his body.

"Duck egg. I've been saving it." She chewed carefully. Koschei tried not to wince. Yaga tilted her head, looking confused for a second, and put her fingers to her mouth. "Something must have gotten mixed in."

Koschei's blood turned cold. Yaga took her fingers from her mouth and drew out a needle. "Now how the hell did that find its way into my eggs?" She looked at him with feigned innocence. She held the needle up in front of their faces, and it wasn't a small needle. The eye of the needle was large enough for Koschei to see her through. Then, she took that needle, and she popped it back into her mouth, crunching it with her legendary iron teeth. With the first bite, Koschei twitched heavily, and his eyes went wide. His age began draining back into him, and he grew older before her eyes, as she chewed noisily.

He sat slumped before her, sweating heavily, pale faced and white eyed. His lips were almost white now, and he whispered, "How did you find it?"

"I always knew, Kass, I have had this in my safekeeping for centuries. It is my business to know things. What a stupid thing for you to have done, both then and now."

With the last satisfying crunch, Yaga crushed the needle between her teeth and swallowed the dust that remained. She took a drink of her black coffee to wash it all down. He slumped further into the chair, his eyes empty and his jaws slack. His skin looked mostly grey now. And then, as suddenly as Kali had, the man became nothing but the shape of a man. The person himself was gone, and what was left turned to black earth. He crumbled away around the chair as she drank her coffee. He might have been satisfied to know that her eyes were wet with tears, but not once did she let any of them escape. She threw the rest of the plate of eggs away.

On the counter beside her egg basket sat a series of egg-shaped matryoshka. The tallest doll was painted with a tree, on a tiny island surrounded by water. The doll next to it, slightly smaller, was painted as a chest. It was followed by a hare, a duck, and finally an egg. Yaga used the last tiny egg to scoop up the dust that remained of Koschei and carefully stacked all the dolls together again. She placed the tree egg, with all its hidden layers, on the counter reverently and walked away.

CHAPTER NINE

The pains in her back and belly could no longer be ignored. She was ravenous, and her belly had been growing by the minute. Whatever she was pregnant with, it was time to find out. She stripped all the bedding from her bed, habit she supposed, as she had no idea what to expect from this odd pregnancy. The pains intensified. She walked through the halls, through her rooms, pacing and pacing herself at the same time. There were no real tricks in this game; babies would do as babies would do, and not much could change that.

The low pain in her belly intensified, but still she walked. There was nothing to be done for it, no one here to help Baba Yaga who had helped so many babies to be born in to the world. She walked until the pain doubled her over and shortened her breath. It was one thing to be on the side helping a woman have a baby, and she thought back now on how matter of fact she had been with all those women. She had told them everything would be fine, to breathe, to push. She had behaved like she was conducting a symphony, rather than directing a woman in extreme pain to experience something more fully, as well as safely. By being too detached, she may have missed the point of the experience over too many generations.

Hours, minutes, months passed, and Yaga paced the floor. Her belly heaved now in three minute intervals, in pains that rippled through her entire body. She sat in her rocking chair, legs braced apart, and rocked with the contractions, feeling her body trying to open to release the child that she held. She felt like she was giving birth to the entire world and wondered if her body could be torn apart. She was filled with wonder at how a child could endure such a brutal introduction to the world. She reflected on how brutal the world could be and realized the process couldn't be more perfect. She felt fierce, she felt powerful, and she felt helpless, rocked by the waves that enveloped her body against her control.

It was at this time that a man walked into the room. Small wonder that she hadn't heard him enter the house, preoccupied as she was, and there wasn't much she could do about it now. She was in the chair rocking when he entered and looked up at him. Sweat poured from her face and her body, her hair loose and long in streaming black ribbons. He was old, older than anyone she had ever seen. She was in the middle of a contraction, gripping the sides of the chair and panting with the effort of it.

"Yaga, let me help."

She couldn't answer at first and didn't even bother to try. Once the contraction passed and she could breathe again, she knew she had limited time. "I don't know who you are or why you're here." She stopped then, because she did recognize him. This was the man from her vision, here when she was at her most vulnerable.

"You have nothing to fear from me." He helped her up from the chair, and she leaned on him heavily. He removed her clothing, gently, and she felt no threat from him. He was much gentler with her than she had been with the women she had helped through this process. She felt shamed that she hadn't shown them a better way, that she had shepherded them through the experience like a herd dog, nipping at their heels when they didn't follow her instructions quickly enough.

He was about to help her onto the bed, and she was trying to tell him that wasn't the way she wanted when another contraction rocked her body. He let her grip him, and he spoke to her in soothing tones. The words that he said didn't matter so much, and she didn't even register them until the pain has subsided. "Stop fighting. The pain you feel is not something to work against. It is the work of your body. However bad it is now, it will pass. Move with it. Envision yourself opening; your child needs your help now."

She stopped trying to control it and instead moved with it. She was the ocean, and she was the sky. She was the earthquake, and she was the tide. When the moment came, it was as if she watched from outside herself. She had never known such pain, but she felt apart from it at the same time. And the man, who looked older than Time himself, helped her through it all. When she focused too much on her body, on the pain, he helped her to focus inwardly. He taught her to see herself as the Universe. Every cell of her body ached to see the task to fruition; every fiber of her body worked toward delivery. She felt everything at once; she saw everything at once; she heard everything at once; she was everything at once. She had never felt so small and so large at the same time.

She pushed when he told her to, but she didn't need him to tell her. She wasn't sure how he knew, because her body knew when it was time to push. And despite the pain, she pushed, with everything she had. How did a woman know how to do this when they had never been through it before? They all had though; every single living person had. They just forget.

She pushed, and when it felt her body would come apart with the pain, she heard a cry. She had heard more babies cry than any other existence in the world, but this one was different. The experience they shared set this baby apart, and already she would lay down her life to protect it. She felt the urge to push again, and her eyes sought his. "The child is fine, but you aren't done yet."

She continued to push, and the baby cried. She felt like she pushed and birthed and bled and sweat for days. She had no sense of time anymore. The baby cried, and she kept pushing. She couldn't even think anymore; her mind was lost to the tides of her body. All she could hear were babies' cries. Yaga wondered if she was hearing every baby she had ever birthed, every mother who had gone on to make more babies—all coming back to her, all her babies in a way.

It was over. The man was still there, and Yaga's exhaustion was complete. Her body was empty, but for one more push. "Once more and you're done." She was positive she had nothing left to push with, but once more the body does what it must, and despite herself, she pushed again. When the afterbirth was freed from her body, that final rush made her feel inside out, an empty husk—less real than she had been before.

She couldn't imagine how women who held their babies for nine months must feel in that final moment when the baby is separated from them. In the peace of that moment, she felt everything slip away. She was drained, so exhausted, she didn't hear anything anymore. She realized that she didn't hear anything at all. She opened her eyes with a pulse of fear, looking for the man who had been by her side. He was still standing beside her; his eyes were not tired, but sad. She did not hear any crying.

She began to tremble. She was an earthquake, a leaf hanging on a tree in a passing storm. "Where? Show me my child. I want to hold—is it a girl or a boy?"

"Yaga," he started, and pressed her hand firmly. "Prepare yourself. Open your eyes, and open them again."

She closed her eyes first, mentally bracing herself. She opened her eyes and held out her arms for the baby she expected to hold, but could no longer hear crying.

"Open them again."

Yaga wasn't sure she was going to able to focus to do anything of the sort, but she opened her eyes again. And there, standing in the room, was every goddess, all the women she had seen disappear. She had seen these women die; she had hunted for them all over the world. They were all here.

"I don't understand. Where is my child? Where is the baby?"

"There is no baby, Yaga. These are your children."

And she saw. She was so much bigger than even she had known. Grandmother Spider had smiled at her, had let her touch the threads of the goddesses who had disappeared but not died. She hadn't understood at the time, how they could have died but not disappeared from the patterns. Morrigan and Kerridwen, Kali and Santa Muerte, Annys and Arianrhod: Hecate, Ariadne, Danu, Freyja, Nyx, Rhiannon, Inanna, Anatha, Anu, Athena, Isis. They were all here; they were all one and the same. They were all individual, and they were all separate. They were all a part of her, and they had all come forth from her. "Yaga is but one of my names," she had said, without knowing how true it was. "All living things are mine own. From me they come, to me they go."

The man who was older than Time helped her from the bed. She stood on shaky legs, still bleeding and trembling. He led her closer to the fire, and she warmed herself. She felt herself stretching, arms and legs, all her muscles, to bring the fire closer to her, to let it warm beneath her skin. It was her bones that were so cold. She closed her eyes again and leaned into him, the only person she had ever accepted help from, and she had no idea who he was.

She stepped closer to the fire, slightly away from her support. She swayed under the emotion of the moment, and opened her heart wider to capture it all. She finally felt warm, after so many years of iron and ice. She opened her eyes again to see all her children, all she had labored for. They were all there still, but fading, and she knew they were being called back to their own homes. She stretched out her hands as though to catch them all and hold them a moment longer. They stretched out in return to her, and she touched fingertips with a few before they were all gone. It was only herself and the man again.

She was still standing naked before the fire, not having noticed or cared. She looked down at herself, at her body, at her hands, and she knew that she was Yaga again, as she was meant to be. She had held all the energy within herself, and now it was all gone. She was depleted and empty and old. She felt a momentary sense of loss, not only for the children who were gone, but for herself. And she understood now, the clutching sense of need that some felt as their youth began to fade.

Yaga knew from experience that youth was fleet-footed, only a temporary sense of identity, but also that it would leave something in its place when it was gone. She was filled again with herself, with her own wisdom and place in the world. She had so much experience to share, and now as never before, love. The man who was older than Yaga, older than Time, stood beside her, and he helped her brace herself through this process just as he had the last. "Let it happen, Yaga. Don't fight the feeling to open yourself, to stretch your body and your mind." She closed her eyes and stretched.

"Stop fighting. The pain you feel is not something to work against. It is the work of your body. However bad it is now, it will pass. Move with it, envision yourself opening, your children need you even more now. You can protect them." And she grew, and she stretched, and she changed. It was like she could see the whole world. She could hear everything; she could smell everything; she could touch everything at once. She wanted to gather them all into her arms, but she stretched out like she was covering them, protecting them with her own body, much as she had while pregnant. Her body would protect them from everything.

She opened her eyes. She was no longer in her home, and there was no fire. There was only the sky and the stars. She was the sky, a goddess stretched out over the world like a dark roof, her belly made of stars, to protect and shelter the earth. She was from Egypt, she was Russian, she was Babylonian, she was Greek, she was Tibetan, she was Cherokee and Armenian, Austrian, Chinese, French and Dominican. She was all things and all times. She was Our Lady of the Stars, and Our Lady of the Sea; she was Stella Maris. She was Gaea, Tiamat; she was the mother of all and the mother of none. She was the Motherland, the sky, the sea.

Her face was like the moon, hair black as night and studded with stars, and she stretched out over everything. The man was no longer with her in person, but she could hear him speaking to her still. She could see everything: past, present, and future. She could see him in her mind, which encompassed all things. He was Chaos, the dark harmony from which all things came and all things returned eventually. From Chaos came the solid world, the water, and the starry heavens. From the tumult on earth, chaos suggested the lack of a pattern, but elevation allowed Yaga a new perspective. Lives may seem to drift without design, but the truth was the pattern was so big, so all-encompassing that no one could see it. But Gaea could see it. Baba Yaga could see it.

ABOUT THE AUTHOR

I've always been passionate about literature and the influence it has on people and culture. I grew up reading voraciously: ghosts, dragons, angels and devils, lawyers, time travelers, monsters and fairies. I took a degree in literature, became enamored with archetypes, and stayed for another, taking a Masters where I managed to focus on Medieval literature and a thesis on alchemy.

Azalee Wolfe

Watch for Azalee Wolfe's next book:

RUSULKA

The oldest stories are not always the prettiest of stories. In some, a mermaid is the spirit of a woman murdered by means of water, creating a vengeful spirit who will lure men to their deaths, out of both revenge and loneliness. Sometimes the mermaid is a girl who drowned herself to release herself from the pain of a lover's rejection. In some stories, women who were blamed for the storms were thrown overboard to try and save the men aboard the ship. What if mermaids are the spirits of these ancient women? She sinks, confined and hidden beneath the waves, dying and undying, until she can teach herself to transform, to overcome. She becomes mistress rather than victim. Only then can she return, bringing the storm with her.

Mermaid legends cross all cultures and all times. Much of legend associates mermaids with misfortune, the cause of shipwrecks and storms. They tend to be temperamental, unpredictable, prone to terrible anger and jealousy. In all of the stories, there are dualities: beautiful and savage, wise and manipulative, seductive and shy. The mermaid is seen as both dangerous and dangerously attractive. If water is a symbol of the subconscious, mermaid stories are about the human psyche. Seek your genuine self; give life to what has been hidden away. Find the treasure that you hide even from your self, but maintain conscious control. It comes with a warning: do not let your depths drown you.

www.azalee-wolfe.ink

www.ingramcontent.com/pod-product-compliance
Lightning Source LLC
Chambersburg PA
CBHW021046130626
46552CB00005B/2044